MAKE ME YOURS

BRIDGEWATER COUNTY - BOOK 5

VANESSA VALE

Cover design: Bridger Media

Cover graphic: Period Images

GET A FREE BOOK!

JOIN MY MAILING LIST TO BE THE FIRST TO KNOW OF NEW RELEASES, FREE BOOKS, SPECIAL PRICES AND OTHER AUTHOR GIVEAWAYS.

http://freeromanceread.com

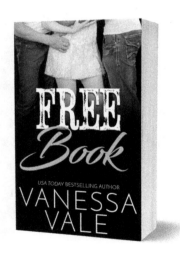

ACEY

"Best sound ever," I said to my assistant, Tessa, indicating the automatic door lock that had just thunked into place.

I settled back into the plush seat— just as comfortable as first class on the plane, but I was on the ground and almost home. What was a slog through

LA traffic after a fourteen-hour flight? I sighed, leaned my head back.

"Even better than someone announcing your name for a walk down the red carpet?" Tessa teased as we settled in to wait for a family of five to finish loading their luggage into the SUV idling in front of us.

"Oh yeah. So much better," I said, tilting my neck from side to side to work the kinks out. "You know I love my fans, but a two-week press junket is enough. So is the batch of paparazzi outside customs. And those rabid fans who don't know a thing about me." I pointed out the window at a bunch of star followers.

"Sounds like somebody needs a massage."

While Tessa investigated the basket of magazines, chocolate and champagne sent by her office, I wearily watched the crowd outside. Undeterred by the tinted windows, my fans jostled elbow to elbow as they angled to capture me on their phones. I was a people-pleaser by nature, but I took petty satisfaction in the frustrated expressions of people who realized they weren't getting anything through the glass. They wanted more from me and I wasn't willing to give it. Not now. Not after the long flight from South Korea, not in my leggings and sweatshirt, my hair up in a sloppy bun. Not when all I wanted to do was crawl into bed for twelve hours.

Airport security finally showed up to clear the walkway. At the same time, the family in front of us finished stowing their luggage and piled into their vehicle. Our car started to move, which I took as my cue to let out a deep sigh and slump down even further. No cameras, no fans. I could be myself.

Tessa chuckled. "So, you want me to book it?"

I rubbed my forehead. "What?

Sorry. I'm exhausted." It was daylight, but I had no idea what time it was. All I knew was that I crossed the International Date Line and went back a day.

"The massage. Do you want me to arrange it? I can make a call and have that massage therapist you like meet us at your house."

My head started to bob the automatic, expected response. Everybody knew being worked over by some big blond Viking with amazing hands was supposed to be the miracle cure to Los Angeles stress, but no. I couldn't even count how many hours I'd spent being kneaded and rubbed since I'd ditched my small-town life as Lacey Leesworth in order to become rising star, Lacey Lee.

None of those massages had done a damn thing. Instead of nodding, I turned my head to look at Tessa, who was

4

thumbing through a stack of tabloids balanced on her lap.

"No. I don't need a massage. I need..." One of the tabloids distracted me and I sat up, reached for the tabloid. "Oh my God. Are they serious? A June wedding?"

Tessa quickly flipped the rag over, but it was too late. I laughed humorlessly and shook my head.

"I'd say I can't believe this, but of course I can. I must have given a hundred interviews in South Korea alone, and all anybody wanted to talk about was my so-called love life."

Love? Hah.

"You know how the media is," she countered, rolling her eyes. Since she worked for a PR firm, she dealt with them twenty-four/seven. "They're hungry for the next big love story. You're the current sweetheart of TV and Chris is—uh, has the potential to be the next big swoony rock star." Her voice changed when she spoke of Chris, the words filled with some doubt. "Of course, everyone wants the two of you together."

Instead of calming me down, it made me grind my teeth. Any mention of Chris did that these days. "Yes, I get the media. I just...argh!" I waved my hands in the air. The gesture indicated all of my frustration with the media, the fans and even Chris.

Tessa winced and patted my leg. "You're burned out. Anybody would be after filming and the press junket. No one imagined the Hunters series would be such a hit. Vampire romance still has a huge following, not only here in the US, but in the Asian market as well. You've been going and going at this pace for five years and know how it is. Let all this stuff go. Besides, it's not like anyone believed you had Elvis' secret baby last month." She was using her familiar placating tone, which was probably the first thing they'd taught her in Celebrity Management 101.

That had been different. Elvis died before I was born. Chris, though, was alive and well—as far as I knew—and thriving in the press of our barely-real relationship.

"'All this stuff', meaning all these lies?" I grabbed the magazine off her lap, lifted it up so I could see my face smiling from some red-carpet event. I recognized the red dress. Paris? Sydney? I couldn't remember. A smaller picture of Chris was in a square in the right corner, big bold type screaming "Wedding Bells or Wedding Hell?" across the top. I dropped it back in Tessa's lap, then stared out the window, watching LA pass by, yet at the same time seeing nothing at all.

"This is Hollywood, Lacey. You're a TV star. Very little about your life is true. If the truth got out..."

Tessa trailed off ominously, shaking a

genuine laugh from me. I shot her an amused glance.

"You say that like I have some kind of deep, dark secret when nothing could be farther from the truth. Like Elvis' love child." I couldn't help the smile that tugged at my lips. "All I do is work and sleep. I couldn't even think up half the things they say I do. My life has been an open book since my first deal, and the paparazzi helped themselves to everything before that. My real name isn't even a secret."

She gave me a look that said it all. She pitied me. Yeah, I had money and fame, but nothing else, and she knew it. She knew what it was really like to be a famous actress, and because of that, she was content to remain behind the scenes, anonymous to the fans and stalkers. When Tessa dropped me off, she'd go home to play tennis or go to the library. Maybe even go to the grocery store with no makeup on. Normal stuff. I hadn't seen the inside of a grocery store in years; I couldn't pick out my own produce without the paparazzi following me, snapping some horrible candid and putting it online and saying I was on a juice cleanse. God forbid I picked out my own tampons; an article about a miscarriage or a post about how the zit on my chin was obviously from PMS would surface the next day.

"I didn't mean it like that," she countered. "But how do you think fans would react if they knew you and Chris weren't their dream couple? Headlines aren't made based on 'casual dating' and 'we hit it off, but there's nothing serious'." Tessa air quoted in all the right places.

I rolled my eyes, sighed. "I don't know. Maybe they'd start reacting to my acting ability again instead of all this... nonsense. What do you think people would say if they knew Chris and I haven't exchanged more than a single text during the past week?"

Tessa got a panicked look. "Don't tell anybody that."

I laughed at her expression. "Yeah, that's what I mean. The truth would ruin my career, which is so ridiculous, I can't even list all the ways. I hate this, Tessa. I don't want people marrying me to Chris and I'm resentful of the PR team for pushing me to go along with this whole stupid charade while I was away."

"Okay. Just hold on." Tessa shuffled all the tabloids aside and angled to face me, tucking one leg beneath her. She had on skinny jeans with wedge sandals, a cute tank top with ruffles down the front. It was obvious she hadn't been on a flight from Asia. "What's really going on? You're way more off than usual. If it's burnout, we can set up a self-care retreat. Self-care is the big buzzword right now anyway. Your fans will go nuts with admiration and the press will run with that."

"The press will start speculating that I'm carrying Chris's baby. Or that I'm in rehab."

I couldn't decide which was worse— fake pregnancy or fake bulimia. Maybe I should go buy some tampons. That would settle one of those things.

Tessa opened her mouth, but then closed it with a rueful laugh. "Okay, you've got me there."

"Mm-hmm. But a retreat does sound amazing." Sighing, I tugged my hair out of the sloppy ponytail, smoothed it out and tied it back again. I'd been all around the world, yet I wanted to get away. Not to a jam-packed schedule full of meetings, interviews, release parties and red carpets. No, to somewhere quiet. No cameras. No phones. No connectivity.

Tessa looked genuinely concerned.

We'd been together long enough that I knew she was actually worried about me, even if only because her job depended on my career remaining stable. The professional barrier kept us from being friends, but since she was the closest thing to one I had in LA—and the fact she'd signed a non-disclosure agreement not to share my secrets—I decided to confide in her.

"You're right. It's more than burnout. I'm lonely, Tessa. It's just me when I'm home and it's even worse when I'm touring. Please don't tell me I have all these 'adoring fans'." I could air quote at key moments, too. "I don't—well, I do want fans. Obviously. But I can't be sustained by the fickle love of billions of strangers, especially since the person they're really drawn to is a fictional character. A series of them." I sighed, tugged at the string on my hoodie. "Oh, you know what I mean."

Tessa nodded slowly, setting her dark hair swinging. "I think I do. So—what about Chris? Would it really be so bad to be more than casual with him?" At my dry look, she wrinkled her nose and laughed. "Okay, yeah, stupid question. He's an arrogant, self-important mess."

Not to mention a user, but I didn't need to tell Tessa that. She was well aware of how my affiliation with Chris benefitted his career. Mine? Not so much. I was already the sweetheart of the big screen. Our so-called engagement was pure fiction, dreamed up by the PR company that represented both Chris and me.

I shrugged. "He's...I don't know. Chris just isn't what I want."

I wanted love, the sweet, simple, uncomplicated kind of love my sister had found. I wanted instant connection. I wanted a guy who wanted me more than anything else. Hot sex, too. Yeah, I wanted that with a guy who knew he was in bed with me, real Lacey.

What good was money and stardom if nobody wanted the real me? The woman, not the star? And Chris didn't even know who the real me was. He didn't care.

Poor Tessa didn't deserve this heavy conversation so I shrugged and gave her a wan smile. "Okay, book me the retreat. Make sure it has plenty of long, hot baths. I only have two weeks between now and the next tour. Let's make them count."

"Yes! That's the Lacey Lee I know and love." Tessa clapped her hands, then whipped out her tablet.

As she fired off retreat options, I picked up the stack of tabloids. The glow of the tablet screen made the headlines seem lurid and too ridiculous for words.

La-Chris was an absurd couple name. Chr-acey was even worse, but at least the sentiment was right. Crazy was just the word for all of this. For the fake relationship I had with a guy I barely knew.

One headline made me huff a laugh. Tessa glanced up. I brandished the paper at her. "Rock4Ever? What is this, a time machine back to the nineties?"

Tessa didn't get a chance to answer. The car slowed in front of my house, which was lit up like Christmas. Trucks and cars alike parked up the driveway and the lawn.

"Holy shit." Tessa leaned over me to look out the window, eyes bugging out. "Is that a tour bus?"

"What's going on?"

Tessa and I looked at each other. At the same time, we both groaned, "Chris."

Nobody else would have the nerve to turn my million-dollar house into a freaking party palace. Especially while it was well known I was out of the country. Or had been.

Music pumped from every window, so loud I could hear it inside the car. As I watched, horrified, three women I didn't know pranced out the front door, stark naked, carrying wine glasses and passing a joint between them.

Tessa made a disgusted sound. "I can't believe this. Stay here. I'm going to clean this mess up and get rid of Chris."

I reached for the door first and waved her back. "No, don't. You go home. I'll handle this myself."

I might not have any control over the media's portrayal of my so-called love life, but I could sure as heck tell one person the truth. If Chris thought he had a right to anything I'd busted my butt to earn, he was dead wrong. This wasn't a relationship, this was a self-centered asshole using my name.

Flinging open the car door, I grabbed

my carry-on and marched right through the pack of drunk groupies. My front door was hanging wide open. That would have been perfect for my dramatic entrance except for one thing.

Chris wasn't there to see it.

The people who were around were either too blitzed to notice me or they just didn't care that they'd been caught trashing my home. They probably didn't even know whose home they were in. And why would they care? Chris's people were all from the rock scene, musicians and groupies. A rager of a party was the norm, even in the middle of the day—whatever time it was. Mine was probably the third house or hotel they'd wrecked this week.

Head pounding from the blasting music and the wicked strobe lights someone had installed, I wandered from room to room. The house wasn't big by LA standards, but it had floor-to-ceiling windows with incredible views. When I didn't find Chris on the first floor, I headed upstairs, avoiding empty beer cans and carelessly strewn panties.

I didn't even bother checking the guest rooms. If Chris had the nerve to invade my house, he wouldn't behave like a guest. Following the trail of discarded clothes and shoes, I walked through my open bedroom door to a sight that would have shocked me at eighteen.

Some blonde I didn't know was on all fours on my bed while Chris pumped away behind her. Up until this moment, I'd walked through the house with a sort of numb sensation, my vision freaking out over the light show, the crazy partying. Now the numbness evaporated and sharp clarity rushed me.

I didn't want this. I didn't want any of it. Not the fancy house I'd purchased because that's what LA stars did, not the famous rocker boyfriend fans thought completed my image. Not the drugs, parties, and endless travel.

I didn't want any of it. I was done. D.O.N.E.

Leaving my bag beside the door, I walked over to stand directly in front of Chris and his groupie, the sound of his hips slapping against a perfect quarter-bouncing ass filling the room.

Chris didn't display an ounce of shame when he saw me. The opposite, in fact. He grabbed his sex toy's hips and jerked her ass against his groin lewdly. If he was caught, he didn't want it to be with his dick hanging out. No, he wanted it buried deep.

He grinned, giving me that drop-dead gorgeous look cameras loved. Tousled blond hair, square jaw, perfect body. Even his dick was good looking— when it wasn't filling up some nameless, faceless chick. He disgusted me. Nothing about him appealed to me—even before I had to stand here and watch him fuck someone else. His personality was narcissistic. He dreams, shallow. So was his behavior. No, he was an asshole and I had no idea why I let the PR people string this along. They must have loved me being in Asia; I couldn't see what the real Chris was like with the Pacific between us.

"This cock's occupied, Lace," he said, his voice deep and yet full of mocking humor. "If you want in on the action, you'll have to ask my lady friend for some tongue."

"Your lady friend." My eyebrows couldn't possibly rise any further. She was no lady and I would bet my house he had no idea what his friend's name was.

Yeah. D.O.N.E.

"You know what, whatever." I tossed up my hands, let them fall back to my sides. "I'm not going to ask. You and your lady friend need to get off my bed before I call the cops."

With one hand, he reached around and cupped a very fake breast. "You wouldn't."

I narrowed my eyes. "Yes. I would." I didn't realize I was shaking until I jabbed my finger toward the door. "Get out. Both of you."

The blonde flipped her long hair back and gave me a dirty look. "Bitch, ever heard of waiting for your turn?"

I held up my hands and took a step back. Then another. "I'm not doing this." And I wasn't referring to getting some tongue.

Turning, I grabbed the house phone off the nightstand.

"For fuck's sake, Lacey." Chris pushed his partner away and looked around the room, condom covered dick glistening. At least he was smart enough to use protection. I wasn't sure if I should gag from the porno in front of me or if I should be impressed he used protection.

"If you're trying to find your pants, they're on the stairs." I thumbed over my shoulder. "You can put them on while you're on your way out of my life."

His shoulders stiffened but his erection flagged. I glanced away. I didn't need to see that. "What did you say?"

"You heard me. I'm not doing this anymore. I won't be associated with you, not even in the tabloids. When your PR firm wants to know what went wrong, you can sort it out."

His lip curled back in a sneer. "Fine. I don't need your stuck-up bitch face to get me where I'm going. I was only into you for the connection, to get the world looking at my band. I've got that now and I don't need you anymore. It's not like you ever put out."

Thank god for that. I had to thank

my busy schedule for once to have kept me away from his dick. We'd done things together—events, dinners, casual parties —but never alone and never naked.

He climbed off the bed, tugging off the used condom and tossing it in my trashcan. "You know what, Lacey? Go ahead, call the fucking cops. Get the press in here, too. Let's make this breakup official."

Out of the corner of my eye, I saw movement in the doorway. I whipped my head around to find someone from the party had already found us. The guy wore a stage crew t-shirt across his narrow chest and a had his phone pointed at me, Chris and the blonde who, instead of scrambling away in shame, had dropped to her knees on the carpeted floor and devoted herself to reviving Chris's limp dick.

"Put that away," I growled.

"Fuck, no. Keep it out. Let's get this

on camera." Chris fisted the blonde's hair and pressed deep into her mouth until she gagged.

Slamming the phone down, I turned my back on Chris and everything else, stopping only long enough to grab my clutch from my carry-on. If they wanted to film a porno, so be it. I wanted nothing to do with it. I wanted nothing to do with him. I didn't need the police. Chris and his party people would leave eventually. The PR firm who'd put us together in the first place would do damage control on the house and my public image tomorrow.

Or they wouldn't. I pushed past the guy in the doorway, who kept the camera on the little sexcapade in my bedroom, down the stairs and out the front door— which still stood open. The fresh air did nothing to make me feel better. As I called for another car to pick me up and settled on the curb at the end of the driveway to wait, I realized I didn't care whether anybody cleaned up this mess or not.

I just didn't care. This was not my life. This was not me. I needed out. Away. I just didn't know where to go.

2

$\mathcal{M}$ICAH

"There's a pretty girl. Go on, gobble it right up. I've got more where that came from. Long as you behave, you'll get your fill."

Behind me, the scuff of a boot preceded an amused laugh. "This one doesn't need buttering up, Micah. I picked out my easiest girl for you."

"That right here is why we're still

single, Colt. I've never met a lady who didn't need at least a little bit of seduction. This filly's no different, are you, girl?"

The horse rolled her big brown eyes and tossed her head as if to tell me to get lost so she could enjoy her apple in peace. After giving the other mare her own treat, I left the pair of horses to munch at the edge of the corral and strode over to where Colt Benson was pulling down the gear I'd need for my mount and the mares my clients would be riding.

The September sun was still warm and I stopped to roll the sleeves of my long-sleeved shirt up.

"Our seduction game's just fine. It's our judgment that's shit." Colt tossed saddlebags my way.

I couldn't argue with his assessment because it was true. Our—yes, our, because we were Bridgewater men, and we'd been raised the Bridgewater way—romantic judgment didn't have a good track record.

My phone vibrated in the back pocket of my jeans. I pulled it out long enough to scan the message, then deleted it.

"She still texting you?"

I glanced at Colt before putting my phone away and grabbing my packing list. "She never stopped. Next time we date a woman, we're using a burner phone until we're sure she's not bat shit crazy."

A month earlier, we'd been ready to hook up with a woman we'd met at a bar in the next town over. She was pretty, fun, sexually adventurous, and not the least bit put off when Colt and I explained the two of us were a package deal. She'd been more than fine with that, at least for the night, and so had we. That was until her husband met us in the parking lot with a bottle of lube, a box of extra small condoms and a webcam. That had kept our dicks in our pants ever since.

I wasn't the kind of man who needed a warm woman in my bed every night of the week, but I also wasn't the type to have extended sleepovers with my hand.

I didn't regret or resent the dry spell. It had helped me clear my head and really narrow down what I wanted for my life. However, one side effect of all that introspection and abstinence was now I could clearly picture the life I wanted and the kind of woman I wanted to fill my days and nights. Not just a woman, a wife. A woman to share our lives permanently. Mine and Colt's. To make a family.

That kind of clarity had brought a sense of urgency that hadn't existed before. Knowing what I wanted, I wanted it now. I wanted a willing woman, one who would crook her finger and we'd happily strip bare and fuck her hard. She'd want it, wild and dirty, with her husbands. Why? Because the woman for us liked it rough, liked it playful and liked it all the time.

I shifted my cock, getting hard at just the thought of the woman for us and what we'd do with her.

Colt ran a hand over the back of his neck, probably thinking about how we'd escaped a bad situation. "Good thing there's no cell reception where you're headed."

Two days of no texts from a crazy woman hoping Colt and I would fuck her while her husband watched—and recorded it. That was a good thing. The price? Riding into the backcountry with a pair of newlyweds. "Hopefully it won't be like that one time where I had to listen to the couple fucking like bunnies. I swear, they needed to go beyond the first big boulder they found." I winced at the not-so-pleasant memory. "Not my idea of a good time."

I wanted to experience that level of eagerness for my mate that I took her bent over the nearest flat —or mostly flat —surface I could find. I wanted passion and commitment, to have a willing, soft woman beneath me. Hell, on top of me would work, too. Even over a damn boulder. Riding my cock while her breasts bounced as Colt took her ass at the same time.

"I'll lead the horses with you to the cabin, then I'm going to enjoy a quiet day on my own. Work on the framing. I'd love to get it closed in before winter. Then I'll settle into my big, soft bed." He grinned, adjusted his cowboy hat. "Sucks to be you."

Shaking my head, I stuffed the last of the gear into the saddle bags, checked it off the list, and pointed my pen at Colt.

"Sucks to be us," I said, ignoring the rest of his words. "We'll be back before dark, but remember, I'm not the only one who'll be sleeping alone tonight. You and I are paddling the same empty boat." I tucked my pen behind my ear and narrowed my eyes. "Unless you've spent these last few weeks reaching a different conclusion than I have."

It wasn't such a far-fetched possibility. While I owned my wilderness business with plenty of clients and nothing but growth on the horizon, Colt hadn't yet gotten to where he wanted to be.

Colt finished securing the horses' saddles and shot me a look across the back of my mount. "What I want hasn't changed since I was ten years old and we made our pact."

I rubbed my chin. "Maybe not, but things haven't happened in the right order."

We were supposed to both be successful business owners, me with the wilderness retreat, Colt with his own ranch. Not that the order of things mattered to me. I believed events came about and fell into place exactly when they were supposed to. Colt, on the other hand, liked things just so. Five years ago, he'd purchased a hundred-acre spread in a gorgeous valley south of Bridgewater. The land was waiting for him—for us and a bride—to settle on, but that took more cash. And a woman. We needed a house, stable, horses and more. And a woman.

In the meantime, he was still working as lead foreman for Hawk's Landing, a guest ranch owned by our friends, Ethan and Matt. He was invaluable to the place; in charge of the vast stables, the maintenance to the property and buildings, the animals, as well as supervising fifty or so non-hospitality employees. He could handle it, being Mr. Stickler that he was, but I liked the wide-open spaces more. I dreaded paperwork and enjoyed sleeping out under the stars as much as my own bed.

"Things happen exactly in the order they're supposed to," he countered. "If I was meant to have my own spread up and running by now, I'd be tending my own horses and we wouldn't be having this conversation. If our woman was out there already, don't you think we would have experienced that lightning moment by now?"

I settled the pack behind the saddle. It had always been said, by my parents as well as Cole's—hell, almost every married male in Bridgewater—that they knew their bride the minute they laid eyes on her. Like a lightning strike. I'd only been almost struck by actual lightning twice in my career—which wasn't much of a surprise based on what I did—but never the "love" kind.

Cole looked over his shoulder at me with a wicked grin. "Besides, I don't know about you, but I'd hate to live my whole life having missed the chance to laugh as you ride off for a night spent sleeping on the hard ground listening to other people fuck."

He guided two horses by their leads toward the newlyweds' cabin. He might not be going with us, but he was supplying the animals from the stables and needed to make sure the guests were happy before we left him behind for our time in the backcountry.

Grumbling at the reminder, I took the pack horse's lead and ambled after him. "You talk a good game, but I'm serious, Colt. This is our time for some real soul-searching. I'm in as much a hurry to experience the lightning strike as you are, but maybe we should hold off another year."

He stopped walking so I could catch up. "And do what for that year? Put on blinders so we're not distracted from our goals by lush tits and a pleasing ass? And what do we do if those blinders mean we don't see her unless she's standing right under our noses? It's not like she'll know she's supposed to be looking for two Prince Charmings. Hell." He ran his hand over his neck again, a sign I knew meant he was frustrated. "Yeah, I wanted my land to be self-sufficient by now, but ranching isn't some damn corporate ladder. There's no formula for paying your dues. You think I'm the one who's got a plan in place, but it's you who worries about it for both of us. Anyway, you hear all about those poor bastards who get to the top and then look around only to realize they're standing on that mountain peak all alone. They were so focused on their goals, they missed out on their life."

"I stand on those damn mountain peaks as part of my job practically every day. I know a woman isn't standing beside me, beside us, better than you."

He lifted a dark brow at me. "It was an analogy, you fucker. I'm just saying I'm as eager as you to find her."

I sighed, continuing on toward the cabin by the creek. "Fuck, sorry. You're right. I shouldn't have questioned you. I know we're both of the same mind and in the same place."

"Is the same mind having our gorgeous woman naked between us, taking one of our cocks in her mouth, the other in her sweet pussy?" he asked.

That hot image flashed through my head. "Her breasts will be a perfect handful and that ass, lush and full to grab hold of."

"To spank a nice shade of pink."

"To train and fuck."

"Damn straight." Colt grinned. "That's why our wife—the woman who wants everything we just said as much as we do—is going to think we're gods in the bedroom."

"Gods? Nah. We might dominate her in the bedroom, but she'll have all the power. The minute she realizes we worship at her feet, she'll know the truth." We were just men, a pair of cowboys who knew what we wanted and possessed the determination to go after it.

3

 ACEY

"Oh, here's a good one. Ahem. 'Lacey and Chris on the Rocks'. But the best part is the visual. They did this stupid stylized O and made it look like a guitar is splitting the O in half. Hang on, I'm texting you a picture."

My phone pinged as my sister delivered on her promise. Tapping the speaker function so I could still talk to her, I pulled up the photo of the tabloid headline and groaned out loud. "Don't these so-called journalists have any self-respect? This is so bad."

"It's barely even the tip of the iceberg," she continued, and I could hear papers rustling through the phone. "I have a stack right here, and every one of them is crammed full of frantic exclamation points and question marks. The type is enormous, like World War Three is starting, not an actress going on vacation. I don't know how long you're going to be able to hide out before some reporter tracks you down."

I stepped out the open back door of the cabin and onto the covered porch. It overlooked the meandering creek that led toward the main lodge. Everything was green, lush. Quiet. Except for the creek, which I listened to all night—at least for the three minutes I stayed awake when I climbed into the plush king-sized bed. It was the best background noise ever. The air was warm now, but the night had been cool. Perfect weather. Heck, perfect everything. No one knew where I was, I had no commitments, no cameras pointed at me. No fans screaming at me. I had a cabin in Montana meant for my sister.

"Fortunately, everything out here is booked in your name. Thank you again, for all of this," I told Ann Marie. "I can't believe you gave up your honeymoon for me." Deleting the text and the awful headline, I went back inside and crossed the small cabin to gaze through the window that looked out over the valley and Hawk's Landing Guest Ranch.

"Oh, don't even thank me. I should be thanking you. While Mama flipped her lid over me eloping instead of going through with that big fancy to-do she planned, she'll stop short of actually killing me when I return from Hawaii once she finds out I did it all for you."

I shook my head, laughing for the first time in days. Our mother wasn't the insane woman Ann Marie made her out to be. She wanted her first child to have the perfect wedding and might have gone a little nuts over it, but to me, none of it was as crazy as some things I dealt with. A few extra guests—and a groom's cake shaped like an armadillo—did not a disaster make. No, a disaster was a supermarket magazine rack full of lies about yourself. I took a deep breath, let it out. I was in Montana where no one could find me. It was too dang pretty to do anything but enjoy the views. I was going to forget about the shit storm waiting for me when I returned to reality and hope the dark hair dye made me a little more incognito.

"So that's the story you're going

with?" I asked. "You knew two weeks ago I was going to have a personal breakdown and I'd need a place to hide out for a week? And because of this, you and Gabe decided to hop a flight to Hawaii and get married there in order to free up the rustic retreat for me? You know if you try to run that story by Mama, she'll demand to know when you're due."

I leaned down to sniff the fuchsia and white flowers in a glass jar. Sweet peas, I thought.

"Oh crap, you're right," Ann Marie replied. "I didn't even think about her grandbaby fever. Hold on a sec." My sister's voice grew distant. "Hey hon, we're going to have to put in a few more hours of baby-making time to make my mother happy."

Gabe rumbled something in the background, followed a moment later by my sister's breathless squeal and a thud that sounded like the phone being dropped.

Okay, that couldn't be any clearer. They might have relocated their honeymoon from this idyllic cabin to Hawaii, but they were still behaving like newlyweds. Fortunately, when I called my sister after being picked up in front of my house—the sex-filled party house —she'd had the perfect place for me to hide out. A week earlier, she and Gabe had eloped to Hawaii, where they were still enjoying an extended honeymoon. Their original trip was supposed to have been at Hawk's Landing Guest Ranch— my mother's choice, not my sister's. Since they'd decided to elope so close to their wedding date, they couldn't cancel and get a refund from the ranch. Not that it mattered to my brother-in-law, whose number of zeroes put my own to shame. He just wanted my sister to be happy, and if ditching a paid-for wedding and honeymoon in order to escape to a tropical getaway made her happy, then no price was too high.

Gabe's indulgent attitude toward my sister worked out in my favor. She'd insisted I take their honeymoon cabin. It was perfect. A quiet place booked under someone else's name, and not even my assistant knew anything about it. After hearing what had happened, how he'd fucked a blonde groupie in my bed, my sister, bless her, had taken charge of the situation as I tried to recover from my life's implosion. She'd made arrangements for a rental car, again in her name, and shortly after our conversation ended, I was on my way to Montana.

It had been less than twenty-four hours since I walked out of my LA house without a word to anybody. In that time, Tessa had sent nearly two hundred messages between the texts, emails and voicemails. Part of me felt bad for leaving her hanging. Another, bigger part—one egged on and enabled by my sister—clung to the fact that Tessa, as nice as she was, was my employee, not the other way around. I didn't owe her or anybody else details of my whereabouts. Until the next professional engagement, which was two weeks away, my time was just that. Mine. And I wasn't going to share it with anybody.

Even if that meant Ann Marie called me first thing stunned by the latest faux news and the claims that Chris had broken things off with me instead of the other way around.

"Shit, sorry!" My sister's breathless voice came back on the line. "You'd think my man would learn some self-control."

"Or that you'd learn the limits to his control," I teased, laughing. Yeah, I was totally jealous of Ann Marie. Not because of Gabe. He was great and all, but he was perfect for her. Not me. No, I wanted my own Gabe, a guy who was my best friend and also my lover. A man who wanted me—no, needed me—with a desperation and longing that only came from love. I wanted a guy to grab me while I was on the phone because he couldn't help himself. "I was just about to hang up and leave you two to it."

"No, no. I'm not finished with you yet," she continued. "But I do have to be quick. Room service is here right now but as soon as they're gone, I have another round to go with the giant cock monster."

"The giant...okay, I'm not even going to address that." I had my hand up as if she could see me showing her I wanted her to stop.

My sister laughed again. "Sorry, I had a few too many mimosas with breakfast. Okay, so listen. No more tabloids. Relax. Enjoy yourself. I emailed you a copy of the itinerary we had planned, but there should be a paper copy somewhere in the cabin. Since we didn't cancel, everything's still on. Massages, horseback riding, all of it."

"Yep." I spun on my bare feet and went over to the small dining table, picked up the piece of paper with the schedule on it, the Hawk's Landing logo at the top. "I found it when I got here. While you're enjoying your fabulous Hawaiian resort sheets and hottie husband's giant cock monster, I'm going to be riding a horse in the Montana backcountry. No wonder you eloped."

Why Ann Marie wanted to ride anything on her honeymoon besides Gabe was lost on me. I walked back to the window, watched a hawk cut through the blue sky.

"Mama thought it would be romantic...or something." She spoke in a tone that made me think she was also rolling her eyes. "I don't know. She suggested we go camping, too, but I vetoed that one. Maybe she thought if she sent us on a honeymoon in a small tent, she'd get her grandchildren even faster. That cock monster and all."

"Okay, you need to stop putting those two words together. Mama and cock monster? How am I going to face her or Gabe at Christmas? Speaking of, call her for me and tell her I'm alive and that nothing in the papers is true."

"Sure."

Movement in the distance caught my eye and I forgot all about my brother-in-law's dick as a long-limbed, swaggering cowboy came into view, leading two horses.

My sister chattered on but I wasn't listening anymore. The closer the cowboy came, the more of his appearance I could make out. He was tall and rangy, broad-shouldered and narrow-hipped. He wore a western style shirt with snap buttons that gleamed in the afternoon sun. And a cowboy hat. Holy crap. He was an honest-to-God, gorgeous cowboy. Hawk's Landing was amazing, having gorgeous cowboys walking around. They could be movie set extras any day.

He was the complete opposite of Chris. Not that I'd ever really been into him—Tessa had more of a crush on him than I ever had—but Chris was pale and while I'd thought he'd been muscular before, the cowboy put him to shame. These weren't gym muscles. The cowboy had earned his physique with work, probably in the outdoors if his tan was any indication. He just exuded... maleness and my ovaries woke right up.

My mouth went dry and my panties got wet just ogling him. From nowhere whatsoever came an image of my fingers dancing up and down those lines of buttons and tearing the shirt open in order to bare a sexy cowboy chest. Hell, yes. If this was a getaway, then my mind could take a vacation from reality.

It wasn't a fantasy I'd ever indulged in before, but I liked the novelty of it. I liked it a lot.

"Lacey? Are you still there?" Ann Marie's loud voice came through the speaker. I didn't remember dropping my hand to my side, but I held the phone up again.

Apparently, hot men made me lose brain cells because I lost the train of conversation with my sister. Shaking my head, I backed up from the window and patted my hot cheek. I glanced down. Yup, my nipples were hard beneath my t-shirt. "You're not going to believe this."

"What?"

I swallowed.

"What?" she shouted.

"The hottest cowboy to ever walk this

earth," I whispered, although there was zero way he could hear me talking about him. He was too far away. "I can see him from my window."

"Oh my god!"

I went to the mirror by the open door —the weather was too nice to be closed in—and glanced at myself. I was startled for a second at my dark hair. It was my natural color, but it had been dyed blonde for my role in the vampire series. I'd assumed it would be for one season, but the show had become a hit and I'd had to keep my hair light ever since.

Until last night. Until I had the driver pull over at an all-night drugstore to buy the new color before dropping me off at the guest ranch. Until I'd spent an hour in the bathroom to change it. The producers could get me a wig for the show. I was tired of the constant touch-ups.

So yeah, new hair color, but the mess

was tangled and back in a sloppy ponytail. No makeup. T-shirt and jeans. Oh yeah, they'd want a piece of this.

"What! Lacey, you dirty girl. Get off this phone and go get him. Take condoms! You're staying in a honeymoon cabin, there must be a full supply stashed somewhere near the bed. And ask him to find a friend. There's got to be more than one hot cowboy in Montana. Maybe even some lube since you'll want to have a fling with two of them."

"Ann Marie Leesworth," I scolded, my cheeks turning hot at what she was insinuating.

"That's Mrs. Townsend now," she scolded right back. "You're a full-grown adult woman who's only had sex in the tabloids in what...years? If you want to take on two hot cowboys, then go for it. And I mean back door action, too."

I didn't want to think about why my sister was pushing me to have anal sex.

There was no way this guy wanted "back door action" with me looking as I was. He was too hot not to have a girlfriend. Or wife.

"He's probably married," I countered.

There was a knock on the open door and I spun about. There I could see the silhouette of a cowboy. It couldn't be the cowboy I'd seen in the distance. Not even an Olympic sprinter was that fast. No, this was another one. And I knew he was a cowboy because his body was big, broad and I couldn't miss the outline of a cowboy hat.

The silhouette cleared his throat, took a step back onto the small porch so I could see him.

Holy crap.

"I'm not married," he said, his voice deep and very smooth.

"Oh my god," I murmured.

The guy I'd been looking at out the window, which, when I tilted my head to the side, was still sauntering my way. Yes, sauntering.

He was dark, while the one who'd surprised the crap out of me was fair. The one in the distance was built like a runner, this guy was more solid. And his forearms? Holy hell, they were tanned and corded with muscle. I wouldn't look at his hands and think about what they could do with them.

"I'm sorry, I didn't mean to startle you."

Startle me? Hell, he'd made my ovaries not only wake up, but pop out an egg. He was that virile.

"That's okay." What else could I say? I couldn't be mad at him since he was going to appear in every one of my fantasies from now on. I stepped out onto the porch with him.

"I'm Micah with Bridgewater Adventures." He removed his hat and held out his hand. Oh yeah, I definitely had a hand fetish. It was warm and his fingers were gentle as he gripped my palm. "I'm here to take you on a ride in the backcountry." He released his hold and turned to look over his shoulder. "That's Colt and he has our rides."

"What's going on?" I'd forgotten about my sister on speaker, even that I was holding my phone. Lifting it back toward my mouth, I said, "I'm going to have to call you back."

"Oh no. Is it the hot cowboy?"

I hoped the porch floor would cave in and there would be a huge sinkhole to swallow me. My cheeks flushed and Micah grinned. His dark eyebrow went up.

"Nope."

Micah's other eyebrow went up, obviously offended I hadn't called him hot.

"I mean, there's um...two of them."

His grin grew as I redeemed myself.

"Two of them?"

"Yeah, and I need to talk to them."

"No, I need to talk to them," she countered.

"No, you don't."

"Lacey Leesworth," she scolded.

Micah frowned, glanced at the cabin number beside the door. "I'm sorry, I'm supposed to take the Townsends."

"That's me!" Ann Marie said.

The other cowboy, the one Micah said was named Colt—a perfect cowboy name—wrapped the horses' leads around the porch railing and moved to stand at the bottom of the steps. He took off his hat and sun glinted off the dark locks.

"This is Colt Benson. He's the foreman here at Hawk's Landing," Micah said as a way of introduction. "He's brought the horses for the day trip."

"Ma'am," Colt said, offering a slight

head nod. He was eyeing me openly and I felt my heart skip a beat.

"Who is that?" Ann Marie asked.

I rolled my eyes. "The other guy I was telling you about," I replied through clenched teeth.

"The other hot cowboy?"

Colt looked mildly surprised by remaining quiet.

"I'm hanging up now," I said, dying a slow death.

"Is that Mrs. Townsend on the phone?" Micah asked, pointing.

I nodded, put a hand to my face, rubbed my eyes.

"That's right," Ann Marie piped in over the speaker. "There's been a little change. My husband and I eloped to Hawaii so my single, very available sister is taking over our trip."

Colt and Micah both looked at the phone in my hand.

I was going to kill my sister. "Ann Marie," I groaned.

"What? You're single and you're very available. And you said they're very hot."

I peeked at the duo who now grinned broadly.

"Would you still like to go horseback riding?" Micah asked. "You don't have to bring the condoms." My mouth fell open as he leaned in, then whispered, "I always carry some with me. But if you're interested in some of that back-door action you were talking about, then definitely grab the lube."

"Did he just say he had condoms? And what about lube? Oh, he's a keeper. Micah, my sister needs to get laid and you and your friend need to help her with that."

Colt cleared his throat. "I'll be joining you, so that can be arranged." He winked, softening his words.

Micah grinned even broader at that

statement and my eyes flared wide at the idea of doing anything with both of them.

I pressed the phone against my chest to stifle whatever else Ann Marie was going to say. "Will you two excuse me for a minute?"

I didn't give them a chance to respond, but I couldn't miss the way they were silently laughing as I spun on my heel.

I closed the door behind me, then leaned against it. Sighed as I pressed the speaker button and put the phone to my ear.

"Ann Marie. I am going to kill you," I hissed, tipping my voice low.

"What? It wasn't as if you were going to tell them yourself."

"Tell them what?" I countered. "Ask them if they're single and would they like to do tawdry and possibly illegal things with me?"

"Yes."

"On a horseback ride?" I laughed at that, the visual, well... "They'll recognize me first thing. They'll want to fuck a star, not the real me."

"They didn't recognize you. I didn't hear any of the usual gasps and surprise."

I didn't respond because she was right. Neither guy looked at me with the slightest bit of recognition. Did they really not know me or were they good actors?

"Not all guys are assholes, sis. Besides, if they did recognize and want to fuck a star, like you said, but you'll be using them, too. Go for it. Fuck the hot cowboys. The one sounded more than ready. Take those big dicks for a wild ride. Use them all night long."

"It's a three-hour tour," I replied.

"Yeah, and look what happened to Gilligan and the others."

I shut my eyes and laughed despite my wanting to reach through the phone and strangle her. I couldn't help but remember the reruns of Gilligan's Island, the 60's TV show we used to watch together as kids.

I gave myself another quick glance in the mirror, groaned. "This is insane."

"Insane is not taking advantage of the situation. If they're nice guys and as hot as you say, go for it. You're a grown woman. Take charge of your orgasms." She laughed. "Or let them take charge of them."

I wasn't sure if I could do what she was proposing. Yeah, the famous star did all kinds of wild things, but the real Lacey wasn't very adventurous. "You're saying what happens in Montana, stays in Montana."

"Sure. You deserve to have a little fun. And a whole lot of those man-induced orgasms. Just jump them on the lunch break." I heard Gabe say something in the background. "Gabe says do those cowboys. Okay, get off this phone and get pulled together. The next time I talk to you, I want details. Lots of them."

"Talking about it with you is one thing. I can't go off and have a middle-of-nowhere fling with two cowboys. Besides, this is their job. I'm a client. I think Gabe has screwed the sense right out of you."

"Not yet he hasn't," my sister said suggestively. "And those two cowboys should go screw the sense out of you."

"Oh, good lord. Okay, I'm getting off the phone, and not so I can pack condoms and lube. If I did something like that and the press found out, it would be a disaster."

She sighed. "Lacey, you're in the middle of Montana, not walking down Hollywood Boulevard. It's condoms. Not drugs. And lube? Hell, if they're as hot as you say, every woman in America expects you to be tag teamed."

"Ann Marie!" I shouted, then bit my lip. Tag teamed by those two cowboys? My pussy liked the idea just fine. Not that I'd ever done something like that before, but I wanted to be adventurous. And those two? I had no doubt they had cock monsters beneath those well-worn, form fitting jeans they wore.

"There isn't any press. No one's hiding behind a tree. That's the whole point of this adventure. Nobody will know if you decide to do something wild."

"People will find out." I frowned. "They always do."

"Yeah, well, I don't care, and honestly, neither should you. I'm hanging up now. You, go wild. And use condoms! Lots of them."

4

OLT

Holy fuck.

When I first saw the woman on the porch, I wondered if the beauty was one of the newlyweds going with Micah. I was surprised her husband let her get dressed. If she were my wife, I'd never let her wear clothes. Hell, I'd never let her out of bed.

And on a day trip into the backcountry? Yeah, her man didn't deserve her if he didn't fuck her over a boulder. I pitied my friend. It would be torture to know that gorgeous body was being fucked...by someone else.

As I tied off the leads on the porch rail, my eyes were glued to her, taking in every inch of her body; from the dark hair, pulled back in a long tail that fell over one shoulder to the hot pink tips of her bare toes and every lush inch in between.

With the sky a bright robin's egg blue and not a cloud in the sky, I was struck by that damned lightning. I was pretty sure it had hit Micah, too. Ironic we'd just talked about it and then...wham.

This woman, fuck. My damn Bridgewater instincts finally decided to kick in and she was married.

She wasn't supermodel stunning,

which was fine by me. I didn't like a woman who was tall like a giraffe and ridiculously skinny. No, this woman ate more than salad because her curves, each and every one of them, were perfect for my hands. The jeans she wore were trim, outlining her long legs, but not too tight. Her t-shirt though, did little to hide her hard nipples. I bit my lip as I stared at those tight tips. She wore a bra, but her nipples seemed to have a mind of their own. She seemed to sense this because she crossed her arms over her perfect chest and flushed a pretty shade of pink.

Instant attraction. Hell, I'd seen pretty women before, but this was... visceral. Lust was definitely there. I was just glad I had the porch railing blocking her view of the front of my pants.

When I started paying attention to the conversation, I picked up on single and available. Apparently, the woman on the phone—not the one standing before us—was the one supposed to be going with Micah but had instead eloped to Hawaii. Instead of getting busy with her new husband, she was matchmaking for her sister. With Micah and me. I didn't stand for matchmaking, but since she was The One and Micah mentioned condoms, then lube, I was all for it. Seemed Micah was, too.

I definitely missed part of the conversation.

I hadn't planned on doing more than delivering the horses for the ride, but there was no way was I framing when she was around and there was mention of lube. And when her sister said she needed to get laid, I was fine with that. A little playful banter was an easy way to assess her willingness.

Her embarrassment couldn't be missed and she politely went back in the cabin, door closed to obviously yell at the other woman. That didn't mean she didn't want to fuck two cowboys on her vacation, but it was obvious it wasn't something she did every day. No, she didn't seem like one to sleep around.

I glanced at Micah.

He just grinned back.

I went up the steps so I was closer to Micah. "Condoms?" I asked, keeping my voice low.

He was grinning as he turned away from the closed door. "You heard the sister. Lacey needs to be fucked. Is that why you decided to join me?"

Lacey. I'd never caught her name. It was pretty. Different. It suited her.

I reached down, shifted my cock. "You can't have her all to yourself. She's...incredible. I want to fuck her, but I want more than that with her."

"Damn straight." He angled his chin,

rubbed his hand over his chin, whiskers rasping. "She's the one."

I agreed and was glad he felt the same way. "Why the hell is the sister playing matchmaker? Lacey must have men falling at her feet."

We were.

The door opened and Lacey stepped out onto the porch. The soft breeze picked up her scent. Peaches? I stifled a groan as I wondered if all of her was so sweet.

"I'm...um, sorry about my sister," she said, her voice tentative. Her cheeks were flushed pink and her eyes met ours, then away. "She's a little bold."

"That's all right," Micah said, putting a hand on the porch railing.

"I'm a little embarrassed," she admitted, refusing to look at either of us.

I stepped closer, ran my knuckles down her arm. "Hey, don't be. There's nothing wrong with a woman knowing what she wants. If it's me and Micah, we aim to please."

When she finally...finally tipped her chin up to look at me, those dark eyes held a mix of wariness and eager mischief.

"You...you don't know who I am, do you?"

I frowned, but Micah spoke. "Up until you shared your name, I thought you were Ann Marie Townsend."

"Should we?" I asked. She wasn't a past girlfriend. While I'd had more than a few, I wasn't that much of an asshole to not even remember what they looked like.

She shrugged. "Nope."

I couldn't miss the way she seemed to relax before our eyes. Her shoulders lost the tension and she gave a small laugh and it made her eyes sparkle. Yes, fucking sparkle. I hadn't used the word "sparkle" to describe anything in my life. Until now.

"I think there's something we need to get out of the way."

Her delicate brow arched. "Oh?"

I nodded, stepped into her personal space. Instinctively, she stepped back. I moved in again and I worked her backward until she bumped into the wood logs of the cabin. "Oh," she gasped.

I placed one hand by her head, the other brushed her hair back from her face. "I'm going to kiss you."

I wanted to give her fair warning, so if she wanted to say no, she could. I didn't kiss—or do anything else—with an unwilling woman, but I knew she wanted it. I saw it in her eyes, the way her cheeks flushed ever brighter. Slowly, I lowered my head, watched her lips part in surprise.

She was so soft, her mouth full and pliant. I flicked my tongue over her lower lip, tasted her. When her tongue flicked out to meet mine, she whimpered. Yes, she was as sweet as I imagined. Her eyes were hazy with desire when I lifted my head. I didn't move, just waited as she collected herself.

"There. No more embarrassment. Your interest is reciprocated."

"Hey, what about me?" I heard Micah say from behind me.

She smiled and I pushed off the wall, let Micah see her, to have his turn.

He crooked his finger and she walked toward him. Ah, sweet and eager to please. With an arm banding about her waist, Micah lifted her up onto her tiptoes for a kiss of his own. When he finally lifted his head, he nuzzled his nose along her jaw, slowly lowered her back to the ground.

"Get on the house phone and cancel the ride," Micah said, his voice an octave lower than before. Yeah, he was as affected as me. And by just a damned kiss.

She frowned, put her fingers to her lips.

"Don't worry, Lacey, we're still going. I don't kiss—or do other things—with my clients. Cancel and then we'll go for a ride."

She looked to me. "I'm off the clock. I was headed home until I saw you. Sugar, go for a ride with us and maybe, if you're still inclined, you can climb on our cocks and go for a different kind of ride later."

Nodding once, she went inside. I heard her talking to the front desk, but I glanced at Micah. He shifted his cock. "Fuck, yes."

I didn't reply since she came back out.

"All right. I'll go with you."

Micah grinned. Broadly. "Ever ridden a horse before?"

"Ever ridden a cowboy before?" I added, with a wink.

She bit her lip—the lip I now knew was soft and plush—glanced away, then back. She lifted her chin and gave us both a saucy smile. "I'm pretty much a city slicker, but I don't mind getting a little dirty."

Holy. Fuck. My cock went from a semi to ready to fuck with that once sentence. Micah cleared his throat. I had no doubt he was thinking the same thing. I looked her over again. Took in every inch of her because I wanted to get her really, really dirty and I knew she'd like it. No, she'd fucking love it.

"Fine. Good," Micah said. "If you're new to this, don't you worry, you'll be in good hands." He glanced at me, giving me the perfect opening.

"That's right," I added. Lightning had struck and she wasn't married. No husband, no boyfriend. She wasn't claimed. Yet. And there was no way in hell I was letting Micah go off into the woods alone with her. The house framing could wait. It was as if Fate had stepped in and given us this opportunity. To make Lacey The One. "Micah and I will ensure you have an adventure you'll never forget."

―――――

LACEY

Whoever invented snap shirts was a genius because I wanted to grab the front of their shirts and rip them open.

Snap.

Snap.

Snap.

Until their solid chests and rock-hard abs were exposed and I could run my hands all over them.

Them. Both guys.

Even after I pushed that thought away, another popped into my head. How many condoms were there stocked in the honeymoon cabin. And lube? Yeah, I might need to toss that in my bag, too. While I'd been embarrassed by Ann Marie and her matchmaking, she was right. The kisses—from both of them!—sealed the deal. Sealed with a kiss! I tried to suppress a giggle at that.

My nipples were out of my control and I had to cross my arms to cover their bad behavior because it wasn't just my ovaries that were standing up and taking notice.

Micah was the fair haired one and Colt was dark. Colt's square jaw was clean shaven, his hair cut short and neat. He was almost a foot taller and a foot wider than me. While he wasn't scary, he certainly was imposing, until his kiss and the gentleness of his hands eased any worry. His piercing dark eyes raked over me in a way that had my skin heating. My lips tingling. While he might be an employee of Hawk's Landing, he was looking at me like a man. A man interested in a woman. In everything he saw.

Micah seemed a touch more easy-going, quick with those ruthless-to-my-panties smiles. While he wasn't looking at me as if I were prey, I couldn't miss the heated gleam. Especially after I told him I didn't have either a husband or a boyfriend.

What appealed to me the most was that they had no idea who I was. No flare of recognition, only heat. No stuttering or surprised pauses. Not even a "you look heavier in person" which I got from some male fans. Nothing. They wanted me. The real me.

When Micah had handed me a short list of items I should bring and I went in to pack them in the small bag he provided, I sat on the edge of the bed. They didn't know who I was.

To them, I was just Lacey, sister of the bride that didn't show. Not the actress who supposedly just got dumped by her rock star boyfriend.

Colt had said they promised a trip I'd never forget. Based on the looks they gave me, the kisses, and Ann Marie's none-too-subtle attempt to get me laid, I knew there was a whole lot of hidden meaning—and lube—involved. They couldn't have missed my hard nipples. I groaned and glanced down. Now they behaved. And they knew I was into their kisses. Both of them. Oh god. Two men.

I shook my head, then looked at the list. They were waiting for me, horses at the ready to go off on a little adventure. Besides the fact I was going with two extremely hot guys, I couldn't get any more off the grid. No phones, no cameras. Nothing. This might not be the retreat Tessa'd had in mind, but heck, when God gave me two hot cowboys, I went horseback riding in Montana.

I stood, grabbed my sweatshirt, raincoat, sunscreen and the other things on Micah's list and got busy. Glanced at the bedside table, took a deep breath, grabbed the condoms and yes, the lube.

5

ACEY

Somehow, I'd made it twenty-six years without getting on a horse. I'd been fine with that, hadn't known it would be remotely interesting. I'd been completely wrong. I was enjoying it a whole heck of a lot. Of course, I never imagined riding between two Marlboro men—minus the cigarettes and ten times the sex appeal—either. That made all the difference. I was practically drooling at the way their strong thigh muscles were blatantly visible beneath taut jeans. Their hips rocked with the gentle motion of the horses and had me wonder what else they could do with them. Not the horses, their hips. And their hands holding the reins? Gah.

I had no idea I had a hand fetish until now. I definitely noticed the lack of wedding rings. I spent the first hour just silently ogling them. I had to hope they were thinking I was just taking in the beautiful scenery. I was, but not the beautiful scenery they were thinking.

I did begin to appreciate the mountains, the bright green valley with spots of colorful wildflowers. The warm sun that was filtering through the fast-moving clouds, the fresh air. The peace.

"Where are you from, Lacey?" Micah asked, breaking me from my thoughts. They'd been quiet ever since we left the ranch, seemingly content without any kind of small talk. Besides some heated glances and Colt helping me up onto the horse with a little more attentiveness than necessary, the kisses weren't mentioned and they'd done nothing else overt.

I turned my head. Micah's cowboy hat was low on his head, blocking out the sunshine, but his dark eyes were on me, waiting.

"LA."

"Never been," Micah replied. "Heard there's bad traffic."

Out here, with the wildflowers and the soft breeze, LA seemed so far away. "Bad traffic, annoying people. Just busy. But there's better weather."

"Than this?" Colt asked, lifting a

hand from his reins to signify the gorgeous day.

I looked up at the sky, saw a bird soar past. "This is spectacular. I bet winters are pretty cold and you're stuck inside a lot."

"Being stuck isn't so bad if you're with the right person."

I shifted in my saddle, thinking about being stuck with Colt. "Are you both from Montana?" I asked, trying to keep the small talk going. I liked what I saw about the two of them, but if I left it at that—their good looks—then I wasn't any better than my fans; lusting after the surface and not knowing the person underneath.

"We're Bridgewater men, through and through."

I'd passed through Bridgewater from the airport. A quaint, small town right out of a western postcard. "Seems like a great place to grow up. Your families are here?"

Micah used his finger to tip his hat up a bit. His face was less in shadow and I could see his pale eyes better. "My parents are in Bridgewater. My brother lives in Helena."

"My parents moved to Texas a few years ago," Colt added.

"You live in town then?" I thought of Ann Marie and our conversation, bit my lip, then bit the bullet and sought the answer I'd been dying for. "With your... with your wives?"

I looked down at my hands, afraid to see their faces. They were quiet. I was an idiot. God, such an idiot!

"Are you asking if we have a woman in our lives?" Colt asked.

I frowned a little, confused by his wording. I shrugged, afraid to say more.

"It's fine. You have a right to know," he added.

I glanced up at him, frowned. "No, I don't. It's none of my business. I apologize. I was trying to make small talk and I... well, should have asked after the weather or something."

The wind kicked up then and I tugged my ball cap lower. I'd put it on earlier to shield my eyes from the bright sun, but it had since hidden behind clouds.

Micah laughed, drawing my attention away from Colt.

"Lacey, we kissed you. We don't do that if we're with someone else. We're not married," he said. "No girlfriend. We've been looking for the right woman to come along."

I nodded. Definitely understanding. If I were Ann Marie, I would have laughed this all off, said some witty reply and moved on. Me? I felt silly. "I can understand that. So...it's warm today."

It was Colt's turn to laugh. "You don't

need to talk about the weather. After the kiss we shared, you can ask us anything."

I bit my lip, my thoughts taking a very naughty turn. Did they always go after the same woman? Did they like it a little rough and wild? Were they as dominant in bed as they seemed to be out? "Anything?"

"Anything," he repeated, this time his tone a touch more serious. "We'll take turns."

I glanced between the two of them, saw their relaxed postures, their easy smiles. They weren't embarrassed as I was, so I let it go. I took a deep breath, smiled. "Sure."

"I'll go first," Micah said. "An easy one. What do you do for a living?"

I bit my lip. I wouldn't lie. While I was enjoying being anonymous, I wasn't going to be something I wasn't. "I'm an actress."

"Movies?" Colt asked.

"No." I didn't do movies. That was the truth. "My turn." I kept my gaze on Colt. The wind was stronger now, stirred my ponytail. I wanted to ask him if he liked a woman on top or if he liked to fuck her from behind—either was fine with me—but no. I stuck with the vanilla question. "You're the foreman at the guest ranch. What does that involve?"

"I oversee all the non-hospitality side of Hawk's Landing. Stables, animals, land."

That was a big job. Tons of responsibility. Based on what I saw of the guest ranch, it was well run and the property was gorgeous. The horse I was on seemed...trained.

"Is this what you always wanted to do?"

"Yes, but on my own ranch. But that's two questions," Colt replied. "My turn."

"No, it's not," Micah countered. "You asked her if she was in the movies."

Colt sighed. I couldn't help the laugh as they fought over me.

"Your acting. Been in anything we know?" Micah asked, then glanced up at the sky.

"Clearly not," I replied. Since they didn't recognize me, they weren't familiar with the Hunters show. "I assume you don't watch TV." Or read the tabloids. I didn't word it as a question and both men shook their heads.

"Too busy and I hate commercials," Micah replied and Colt agreed. "With my company, I'm outside all the time, even in the winter."

Made sense. I knew a lot of people who didn't watch TV, including myself. They streamed movies, maybe. "Well, I'll have you know I'm a very famous actress."

Micah tilted his head, studied me. I told the complete truth. While the tone may have been construed as sarcastic and meant to come across as a total lie even though it was completely true, he seemed to be deciding something about me. And it had nothing to do with being a famous actress.

"Good for you." That was all he said.

My mouth fell open and I wasn't sure what to think. "That's it?" I asked. I couldn't help it. "You don't want to know about Charlize Theron or if I have a fancy car?"

"Is that your question for your turn?"

I huffed.

"Lacey, we want to know about you. Charlize Theron seems like a nice woman, but why would we be interested in her when we have a beautiful woman between us? When we know what you taste like?" My mouth fell open at Micah's response. My nipples hardened.

"And a fancy car?" Colt asked. "This is Montana. A fancy car won't last the mud season. What you need is a pickup truck. If you said you had a dually F-350 king cab, I'd say I was in love."

I laughed. "With me or the truck?"

"If you were in the truck, I'd keep you forever."

By the look in his eye, I had a feeling he wasn't being sarcastic. He was dead serious. I cleared my throat and looked to Micah, although the way he was staring at me wasn't any less intimidating. "Besides taking women on horseback rides, what else does your company do?"

"Camping. White water rafting. Climbing. Adventure trips. We partner with friends of ours who have a helicopter company in town to take people deep into the backcountry. Heli-skiing in the winter. The list is endless since we do custom trips."

"If you do such wild adventures, why do this simple ride with me?"

He looked up at the sky again. "At

first, it was a two-day camping trip, but I think it was your sister who called and changed it to a simple trail ride."

I nodded, remembering my sister's lack of interest in spending any time in a tent, even with Gabe.

"It's easier for Matt and Ethan—our friends who own Hawk's Landing—to hire out special trips than to have someone on staff." He glanced at the sky again, which had me looking up, too. "Weather's coming in."

"So, you don't kiss all your clients?"

Micah's gaze shifted from the sky to me and that steamy gaze had me licking my lips. "My last clients were a bunch of guys who were friends in college, thirty years ago. I took them fishing on blue ribbon water. I definitely didn't kiss them, and I didn't want to share them with Colt. I don't kiss any of my clients, Lacey. Remember, this trip isn't on the books anymore."

The wind whipped my ponytail into my face and I swiped it back.

"We only want to kiss you," Colt added, his voice deep and insistent and I felt those words throughout my body.

"A storm's coming in," Micah said. When I turned to look at him, his gaze was once again looking up.

I hadn't been paying much attention —especially since we were talking about kissing—but the wind was starting to blow and thick, gray clouds had rolled in. I could no longer see the tops of the mountains and it had gotten darker. A rumble came from the west. "That was ridiculously fast," I commented. I'd never seen a storm roll in like that.

Micah looked past me to Colt and I could tell they were communicating without words.

"What's the matter?" I asked, glancing between them. A strong gust of wind almost blew my hat off and I put my hand on top of my head to hold it in place.

"We're up in the mountains. Bad weather can happen quick. Catches people unprepared. It's not safe out here. We have to get to shelter."

I glanced around. We were out in the middle of nowhere, two hours from the guest ranch. "Where?"

A loud clap of thunder cut through the sound of the wind. The temperature dropped and goose bumps rose on my bare arms.

"One of the remote cabins is on the far side of the lake," Colt said, pointing. His horse shifted and he leaned forward and patted his neck.

"Occupied?" Micah asked, glancing up. When I looked at the sky, I saw thick, black clouds. I was no expert, so I had to wonder what he was seeing.

While Colt shrugged, he said,

"Doesn't matter if there are guests. Not in this weather."

Micah looked to me. "We need to get indoors. Hawk's Landing has several remote cabins for guests and that's the closest shelter. You don't have to worry, we'll take care of you."

I nodded, believing him. I had no doubt they knew what they were doing. All I knew was to stay away from trees and not swing a golf club in a storm. But that was civilization.

"Obviously, it blew in fast, and it probably won't last long, but we have to hurry." Colt spurred his horse into motion and took off as I pressed my heels into my animal's flank. He started plodding along at the same slow pace as usual, but I had no idea how to get him to go faster. I nudged him again and wiggled my hips, but his pace didn't change. Did he have only one speed? "I don't know how to ride fast!" I shouted into the wind, glancing wild eyed at Micah.

Colt stopped and with expert precision, turned back to me. Before I could blink, Micah scooped me up and off my saddle with an arm banded about my waist. "You'll ride behind me." He pulled me onto the back of his horse, settling me behind his saddle. "Wrap your arms around me and hold on."

I did as he said, shifting my hips so I sat comfortably, then hugged Micah. Tight. Colt grabbed my horse's lead.

"We need to hurry. Okay?" Micah asked, looking over his shoulder at me. I nodded, then leaned into him as the horse started to move, at a much faster pace than before.

One of his hands came down on top of mine on his lower belly, gave them a squeeze.

The hard pounding of the horses' hooves made it sound like a stampede. I felt safe knowing Colt was beside me as I held onto Micah, felt the warmth of his body, the muscles shifting and playing in his back as we moved.

"The rain's coming."

No sooner did he say that than the first fat drops fell. Then came the downpour. It was as if God had turned on a faucet because we were drenched within seconds. Micah gripped my arm impossibly tighter as if he were trying to shield me, but it was no use. I was soaked through within seconds, except for where our bodies touched.

Micah cursed, then said, "Don't be afraid. You're safe with us."

Yes. I was. I wasn't scared at all. In fact, this was exhilarating. I felt like a damsel in distress, saved by the cowboy in white. But I had two of them. My nipples were hard, this time from the cold rain, but they ached because of the man in front of me and the sight of Colt ahead of us, perfectly at ease on his trusty steed. I smiled, then laughed into the rain at my fanciful thoughts. A TV script writer couldn't come up with anything better than this.

6

ICAH

Colt rode ahead to the cabin to see if anyone was there. By the time I rode up, hopped down and helped Lacey off the horse, he'd come back out, grabbed the reins of his horse and mine.

"Empty," he shouted over the pouring rain. "Get inside."

With a hand on her waist, I ran with

Lacey up the two steps and onto the small porch and out of the rain.

"What is this place?" she asked, taking off her hat. The tip of her ponytail dripped water down her back.

"Hawk's Landing has several cabins in the backcountry," I said loudly since the rain pounded the tin roof. Removing my own hat, placing it on one of the two Adirondack chairs. "Guests can hike or horseback ride up here, spend the night."

Colt had left the front door open and she peeked inside.

"This is not roughing it," she commented. "If Ann Marie knew about this, she wouldn't have canceled the overnight."

Lacey was drenched, her jeans stuck to her legs, her t-shirt wasn't transparent, but it didn't hide anything. I could clearly see the shape of her breasts, even the little bumps that circled the hard tip of her nipple. It clung to her belly and I couldn't miss her curves—a narrow waist and gorgeously broad hips.

"I've heard it called glamping before." When she frowned, I continued. "Glamour camping. There's no electricity or running water, but it should be well stocked."

I hadn't taken guests here before, but to others dotted in the back corners of Hawk's Landing's property. The cabin was nestled in a clearing at the edge of a crystalline lake. The porch chairs would have a perfect view of the mountain peaks in the distance, if not for the downpour.

The log cabin wasn't rustic at all. Matt and Ethan had spared no expense. While small, just one room, it had windows that faced the lake. If it was like the others, there was a king-sized bed, a comfortable couch and a small kitchenette with table and chairs. A small propane tank gave the cabin heat, lamp light and a small stovetop to cook food. Those were the basics, but it also had high thread count sheets, a plush mattress, thick rugs on the floor and even thicker blankets. The only inconvenience would be the lack of a bathroom. There was a quaint outhouse behind the cabin, with a wooden door with a moon carved into it.

Colt came around the side of the cabin and up the steps. "The horses are in the lean-to. I took off the saddles so they're fine for now." He turned to Lacey. "You're freezing. Inside, woman."

He held out his arm so she'd enter first.

I closed the door behind us, went to the small heating unit in the wall, turned it on.

Colt went to a dresser, opened one, then another, grabbed towels, tossed one to me.

Lacey stood before us watching, arms crossed, all but shivering.

"Let's get you dried off," I said. Taking her cold hand in mine, I wiped down her arm with the soft, white towel. Colt began to dry her other arm.

"Wait," she said, staring at the glossy wood floor we were dripping on. I watched as she bit her lip, then shivered. We stopped and I flicked a gaze at Colt, worried we were being too forward. But when she looked between us with her teeth pressed into her lower lip, then grabbed the hem of her t-shirt and worked it off—not very easily since it was sodden—I let those worries go.

She took a deep breath and I watched as her breasts rose, then fell, inside the cups of her lacy pink bra.

Holy. Fuck.

"Am I crazy to want you both?" she asked, her voice soft. She took a deep breath, then rushed on. "I mean, I'm a professional woman. I should know what I want and take it. Right? I'm not sixteen. My sister made it more than obvious I've been through a...a dry spell. I shouldn't be nervous. Embarrassed, maybe, but not nervous."

I dropped to my knees before her, looked up her delectable body to see her dark eyes full of desire and a fair amount of confusion. A woman shouldn't be wasting her time debating if she should go after what she wanted sexually. If she wanted a hot fuck with two cowboys, she shouldn't have to think about it. We were here to have fun with her, make her feel good, to learn everything there was about her. While she didn't know we had long term plans with her, she didn't need to be afraid of us. No, we wanted her empowered. Bold in her passion.

"Hell, no." I leaned in and kissed the damp skin of her belly, then looked up at her, the full curves of her breasts...right... there. "This...us, there's something here and we want to explore it with you."

Colt's hand slid up her back and he deftly undid the back clasp of her bra. Kissing her shoulder, he slid the strap off one shoulder and it fell easily off the other. Lacey let it slide off her and drop to the floor.

Colt's breath hissed out at the sight of her hard nipples. They were like ripe berries, bright pink and ready to be tasted. I only had to lean in a few inches to take one into my mouth, to feel the firm press of it against my tongue and the roof of my mouth. And when I applied light suction, her hands came to my head, tangled in my hair. Tugged me closer.

Colt cupped her other breast and it didn't fill up his big palm, but it was high and firm and I was content being on my knees before her all day. But it seemed she had other ideas.

"More," she gasped.

I pulled away, watched as Colt leaned in and kissed her, his thumb sliding back and forth over her nipple. I got to work, undid the button on her jeans, slid down the zipper. I could see a hint of matching pink lace of her panties and my cock was taking charge. With my fingers at her hips, I tried to work her pants off, but they were too wet.

I growled and stood, all the while putting my shoulder into her belly and tossing her over my shoulder to carry her to the bed. Dropped her on it. Colt had stepped back and moved to the side of the huge mattress, grabbing decorative pillows and tossing them out of the way.

Leaning forward, I tugged at her pants again, worked them down her legs until they tangled around her ankles.

With a quick glance at Colt, who seemed as impatient as me, we each grabbed a foot, stripped off her sneakers and socks, then together we got the jeans off her.

Laying before us on the soft bed was an almost naked woman, only her wet, pink lace panties kept her decent. The rain was pounding on the roof, thunder rumbling in the distance. "You're alone with us, sugar." My gaze roved over her body, from her lust-filled eyes to her upturned breasts, narrow waist, broad hips, long legs. Every inch of her pale skin was perfect.

"We're at your mercy," Colt said. "What are you going to do about it?"

———

LACEY

He tossed me onto the bed. I had to

admit, being manhandled by a cowboy was the hottest thing ever. Well, no. Now having the two of them looming over me, their wet shirts clinging to every inch of their rock-hard chests and abs, was the hottest thing. I had a feeling I'd be updating my Hottest Thing status minute by minute, so I stopped thinking. Just decided to act. They wanted me. I couldn't miss the thick outlines of their cocks. And they were big. I licked my lips, then pushed up so I was on my knees before them. Even being up on the bed, they were still taller.

"I can do whatever I want?" I asked, a smile turning up the corner of my mouth.

Colt nodded, his gaze locked on my body.

"Then you're wearing too many clothes," I said.

Micah lifted his hands to his shirt and I shook my head. His fingers stilled.

"Let me."

I moved closer so my hands rested on his chest. Glancing up, I looked into his pale eyes. They were just as dark and stormy as the weather outside, his wet hair a few shades darker. Droplets of water fell from the longer locks and onto his shoulders. Just as I'd wanted since the moment I laid eyes on them, I grabbed hold of the front of his shirt and tugged.

The snaps gave, just as I expected. My mouth watered as each inch of his chest was exposed. A smattering of light hair was on his chest. It tapered into a narrow line that traveled to his navel. As Micah shrugged out of the shirt and let it fall to the floor, I saw the line continued into his jeans.

I took a moment to savor the sight and I was thankful he remained still to let me stare. Blatantly.

Then I looked up at Colt. He was

waiting expectantly. "I don't want you to feel neglected," I said, with a fake pout. I moved my knees so I could grab the front of his shirt and tug it off. Soon they were both bared to the waist.

"Oh, my."

I grabbed the towel in Colt's hand—I doubted he even knew he held it—and began to wipe them down, taking my time and studying ever lean muscle, finding an old scar, watching the way their muscles tensed as the backs of my fingers brushed over their lower bellies. I climbed off the bed, went around behind them to take in their backs.

Hello! Broad shoulders and lats like bat wings. I rubbed the towel over them in slow admiration. As one, they turned, faced me. "Our backs are dry," Micah said with a wicked gleam. "What's next?"

I glanced down. "I don't think I'll be able to get those pants off myself." Not only was it hard to work wet denim off, but they both had on rugged leather boots. Not only that, but I wasn't sure if I could get the pants past those huge hard-ons.

Colt toed off his boots, one then the other and got his pants and boxers off pretty darn quick. Micah wasn't too far behind so they stood before me. Naked. Like completely, totally, gorgeously naked.

"Holy shit," I whispered as I ogled. Yeah, I totally ogled. I'd seen some cocks in my time, taken a ride on a few, but these? Wow.

These were big and thick and long and everything else a woman wanted. While Colt's was a ruddy red with a broad crown, Micah's was longer. They should be proud of them—I was for them and I was eager to get my hands on them. In fact...

"One for each hand," I said as I took

hold. Micah startled and Colt hissed out a breath.

Micah's hand came down and covered mine. "Harder, sugar."

Colt grunted, did the same, showed me how to move up and down his length to please him. "Definitely harder. I like it a little rough."

I flicked my gaze up to his, then with a moment of boldness, I dropped to my knees before then. "Who's first?" I asked.

While they were both hot cowboys, they were so very different. One light, the other dark. One broad, the other leaner. Intense and easy-going. They were like polar opposites and yet, I wanted them both. My mouth watered to compare their tastes, the feel of them filling my mouth, my throat.

It was Colt this time who leaned down, picked me up and tossed me on the bed. "Who's first?" he repeated.

I bounced once and Micah's eyes

were on my breasts as they swayed from the movement.

"The lady is always first."

My feet were on the bed, my knees bent. I felt far from ladylike.

Each of them grabbed an ankle, tugged me down so my butt was at the very edge of the bed. Colt worked my panties down and off, but they got caught on my ankle. Neither seemed to notice since their eyes were glued to my lady parts. I had a feeling those were the ones who were first.

"Last chance, sugar. Tell me now if you don't want my mouth on your pussy because once I get a taste of you, I'm not sure if I'm going to be able to stop."

7

*L*ACEY

Oh. My. God. He was a dirty talker.

"Colt likes pussy," Micah commented as his friend dropped to his knees between my parted thighs.

Since I didn't say anything—why would I?—Colt didn't wait a second longer and put his mouth on me. His tongue to be precise, and in a very expert way. I arched my back and cried out at the hot feel of him.

"Me?" Micah continued, as he moved around to the side of the bed, put a knee on the mattress and leaned over me. While Colt used his thumbs to part me, then slid a firm tongue from my entrance and up to my clit, I had a hard time focusing on Micah's blue eyes. He smiled. "Like that, do you?"

I nodded and gasped as Colt flicked my clit. My skin wasn't damp from the rain any longer. No, it all just rose off of me as steam, I was that heated, that turned on.

Micah's eyes raked down my body, took in Colt's dark head between my thighs. "I'm a breast man." He lowered his head, took one nipple into his mouth, laved and suckled it. He lifted up enough to fan his breath over the wet tip. "Well, T and A. I love tits and I bet I can make you come from me playing with them alone."

"I'm not moving away from this pussy," Colt growled.

Somehow, the idea of them almost bickering over me made me smile. But then Colt did something with his tongue and Micah pinched my nipple. I groaned, not sure if it was from his dirty words or from Colt's ruthless and fabulous attention.

"But I also like a lush ass. Spanking it, fucking it."

Double dirty words. Fuck. "I'm going to come," I said, my one hand tangled in the soft blanket, the other gripping Micah's knee.

"We would never hurt you, sugar," Colt said as he kissed a wet line along the inside of my thigh. "But we like it a little rough sometimes."

"I like rough," I breathed, then

pouted. "But you're not being rough, you're being mean."

A dark brow went up and he grinned, my arousal slick on his lip and chin. "Oh?"

"Make me come," I said, doing a great ab crunch and reaching his head to pull him back to my pussy.

Of course, he didn't do as I wanted, only kept himself a few inches away from where I wanted him and continued to grin. "Bossy, aren't you?"

I flopped my head back on the bed and groaned.

Micah leaned over me. A drop of water fell from his hair onto the bottom curve of my right breast. He leaned down and licked it up. "This time, you'll get your way. Next time..."

He didn't finish the words, at least I didn't think he did. Colt resumed his very ardent attentions on my clit and all brain power sizzled away. My thigh muscles clenched and my back arched. It was when he slowly slid a finger into me, then curled it, that I came.

And I wasn't quiet.

No. I bucked and grabbed, screamed and cried out their names. God's, too.

I'd had orgasms. Vibrators, even my fingers worked. By myself or with a guy, I'd always had to touch myself to go over the edge. I never once climaxed by a man's efforts alone. Perhaps Colt was just that skilled with his tongue or that Micah was distracting enough that I wasn't worrying if Colt thought I looked funny down there or if I wasn't wet enough or if it was taking too long. I wasn't thinking about much of anything. They were too good at...well, making me feel good.

No, that wasn't strong enough for what they made me feel. Hot. Wild. Uninhibited. Beautiful. Blissfully sated.

A huge grin split my face as I stared up at the ceiling.

Colt rose to his full height, leaned down and placed his hand by my head. He wiped his mouth with the back of his free hand as he stared down at me. "Why do you look so smug?"

"You're my first."

He stared down at me with such intensity. "You're a virgin?"

I rolled my eyes. "No, but you're the first guy to...to get me to come."

He grinned then, clearly quite proud of himself. "So the guys before—"

"Obviously didn't know what they were doing."

Micah grabbed my far hip, rolled me toward him so I was on my belly, spanked my ass. I gasped, felt the sting, then the heat. I wiggled away, only to have Colt give me a swat, too.

"Ever been with two guys before?"

I looked over my shoulder at Micah, shook my head.

"Ever told a guy how you liked it?" Colt added, caressing the heated flesh where they spanked.

I bit my lip, thought about it. "No, I guess not. It's just been...vanilla."

"We don't need whips and blindfolds to get you off, sugar. But some rope?" Colt whistled through his teeth. "I'm a world champion roper. Might be fun to tie you up instead of a calf."

When I tried to roll back, he grinned and hooked an arm about my waist. "Got those condoms from your cabin?"

I flushed then, which was ridiculous since he'd had his face buried between my thighs and I was now naked with my butt up in the air. He couldn't see any more of me if he had a miner's lamp on his head. And yet the mention of condoms had my cheeks heating.

"In the little bag Micah gave me."

Micah moved to retrieve the bag and I turned my head to watch him. It had been dropped carelessly by the door and I couldn't help but enjoy the flex of his naked butt muscles as he shifted to pick it up. He pulled out a long string of condoms. I hadn't paid much attention to them, but I had to wonder now if they'd fit because Micah and Colt were big. Everywhere.

He returned to the side of the bed, ripped off a packet and tossed the rest on the bed. "Good thing I have some packed, too. This won't be enough."

I glanced down at the long strip. There had to be at least six. Not enough?

I clenched my inner walls at the idea of being taken by these two that many times. And then some more.

Once it was rolled on all the way, Colt moved out of the way and Micah stepped in behind me. The thick length of him sliding down my heated—and very sensitive—core.

I wiggled my hips, hoping he'd settle right where I wanted him. Colt may have gotten me to come, but I felt empty. And these magnificent cocks would fill me right up.

"Please," I begged. "But go slow to make sure it fits."

"Ah, sugar. I love the flattery, but you've already got us naked," Micah said, sliding very, very carefully into me. My eager muscles stretched and clenched around every inch of him until I felt his hips press against my sore butt.

"Oh god," I murmured, curling my back like a cat. He felt so good.

Colt gave a small huff of a laugh as he settled on the bed, pillows at his back and me at his front.

And by front, I meant very large, very erect cock. It was a few inches in front of me and I had to look past it and up to see Colt's wicked grin and heated gaze.

"Still want a taste?"

It was hard to even understand his words because Micah slid back out at the pace of the Ice Age. I whimpered, shifted.

"I can go faster now, sugar?" he asked.

I didn't turn my head to look at Micah, just kept my eyes focused on Colt.

"Yes." The answer was for both of them. Yes, I wanted Micah to fuck me faster. Yes, I wanted to taste Colt's cock. I wanted to lick up that little bead of pre-cum at the tip. And the way he gripped the base of it and held it for me, he wanted me to do it, too.

I leaned forward and licked him like an ice cream cone. The salty drop coated my tongue and I wanted more. I wanted all of it that I knew filled his large, heavy balls.

The bed shifted as Micah moved out of my way. I'd never taken two men at once, never even considered it. But now, wow. Now, I had no idea if I'd be able to go back. It was just so much...more. Or maybe it was Micah and Colt.

Colt's big hand gently cupped the back of my head as Micah's palm settled on my hip. Wet sounds of fucking filled the room. I was practically dripping, making it easy for Micah to take me. And my licks and sucks on Colt's cock only added to it all. Colt was breathing hard and Micah gave a small groan when he angled his hips, learned what made me gasp.

The more Micah made me feel good, the more I took Colt into my mouth. I was going to come again. I could feel it now, knew the difference between touching myself and having these two get me off. But Micah's cock stroked places inside me that had never been touched before. I had no idea how that was possible, but the spot, just inside, his big head stroked over once, then again, before plunging all the way in. Over and over until I was gripping the blanket and practically had Colt down my throat.

Colt hissed out a breath and tugged me off him by my damp hair. "I want to come in that pussy, sugar."

I clenched down on Micah at the thought, which made him grip my hip and groan. The motions of his hips shifted to erratic. "Shit, talk dirty to her again."

I grinned, realizing the power I had over Micah, the thrill that I was making him mindless.

"What? That I've got the taste of her pussy on my tongue and can't wait to get my dick in it? Or is it that I love watching her perfect tits sway as you get fucked from behind?"

The pleasure that had been building, that made my skin slick with sweat, my nipples pebble and brush against the soft blanket, became too much. I tossed back my head, eyed Colt as the stunning heat overwhelmed me. Then I closed my eyes, tightened my muscles and gave over to the scorching heat Micah was wringing from me. This time, I didn't scream. No sound came out of my open mouth.

"Beautiful," I heard Colt murmur and Micah's fingers dug into my hip. He slammed into me one last time, growled and I swore I felt the heat of his seed through the latex barrier.

As soon as I felt Micah pull out, I was flipped over, spun around as if I weighed nothing. I opened my eyes to watch a very eager Colt settle me in front of him, bringing one of my legs across his body and to his hip so he knelt between my parted thighs. He didn't take his eyes off of my pussy as he grabbed a condom and slid it on.

"Ready to come again?" he asked. His hips were tucked under, his cock jutting from between his powerful thighs and beneath washboard abs.

I was sensitive and sated. "Two orgasms are twice my usual. I'm...I don't know if I can take any more pleasure."

Colt was not to be deterred. "Say no because you don't want more, otherwise, we'll make you come until you pass out."

Oh god.

And with his wicked grin, he tugged my hips so I slid up his thighs and pulled me right onto him. My back was curved up off the bed and the angle was... "Oh. My. God."

I saw Micah toss a tissue covered condom into the waste basket and come back to the bed. "You'll come again, sugar, or Colt will have his feelings hurt. You don't want that, do you?"

I shook my head, looked up at Colt as he began to pick up his pace. He dropped forward, landing on his hand and looming over me. Sweat dotted his brow, the tendons in his neck stood out. A hand came between us and he brushed my clit. So gently, in complete contrast to the way he became unrestrained.

I gasped. The slightest touch and I was so close. How did they know exactly what I needed?

"How many times do you think I can get you to come with my cock deep in your pussy?"

He worded it as a challenge and the intent in his eyes and the expert flick of his fingers told me I was going to be unconscious very soon.

But he didn't do swirls or circles over my swollen flesh. No. He narrowed his eyes, thrust his hips deep...and his fingers pinched.

The sharp bite of pain on my clit morphed into the most incredible orgasm of my life. A full body experience. My nipples throbbed, my toes curled, my skin bloomed with perspiration, my breath was trapped in my lungs. Colors flashed behind my eyelids. I was primed. Easily orgasmic, it seemed. I just needed to be eaten out and then fucked by two men and I'd come like a porn star.

When I stopped thrashing on the bed, calling out Colt's name, he said, "That's one."

"That was three," I panted, surprised I could do any kind of math at a time like this.

"Oh, sugar," he breathed, leaning down to nip at my neck, nuzzle behind my ear. His hips slowed, but didn't stop.

"My mouth on you was just warm up. Priming the pump, so to speak."

"And the one I gave you I get the credit for," Micah said, clearly proud he'd gotten me off.

I shook my head, looked up at both of them. "It's too good. I don't think I can do that again."

Micah stroked my hair back from my face. It wasn't really wet anymore from the rain, but damp with sweat.

"You can and you will," Micah commanded. I had no choice but to take the orgasms they were going to give me.

Colt began to move then, expertly rolling and thrusting, pushing one of my knees back toward my chest. "Here comes number two."

"Oh god." My eyes fell closed, I gripped the bedding and held on for the wild ride to come.

8

OLT

"What time is it?"

Lacey's voice had me turning.

The storm had cleared out after an hour, as quickly as it blew in. In its wake, everything was wet, the air cooler and the sky crystal clear. I was in the open grassy area between the cabin and the lake practicing with my rope, enjoying the view, the quiet.

Hell, I was enjoying the lingering feelings of fucking the woman of our dreams. When I'd pushed Lacey into her third orgasm—with my dick deep inside her—I'd gone over with her. The pleasure had been too great to hold off and I'd come on a growl, my mind going blank and there was no question I went blind for a minute or so.

Lacey was perfect. In bed. There was no doubt the three of us shared intense, amazing chemistry. But that wasn't all I wanted her for. She wasn't a buckle bunny on the rodeo circuit. Hell, she wasn't like any woman we'd ever had before. But we barely knew her. That would change.

I wanted to know everything. Her favorite foods, if she liked gel or mint toothpaste, where she grew up, where she got the scar on the inside of her left knee.

We'd just been waiting for her to

wake up. When we said she'd black out with pleasure, we'd been slightly exaggerating; two men who believed their prowess in bed could render a woman unconscious.

With Lacey, we'd done it. I'd recovered enough to pull out and tend to the condom and she'd been asleep by the time I'd returned from the waste basket.

And stayed that way, until now.

I turned and looked at her, standing on the porch wearing just my snap shirt. Holy fuck, my cock got hard again.

"Around eight," I guessed. This time of year, it stayed light until almost ten, but the sun was gone from sight much earlier than that.

"I slept a long time. I'm still dealing with jet lag. Sorry."

I coiled the rope into long loops in my hand and walked toward her. "What are you sorry for?" I asked.

She'd tugged her hair from the ponytail and it fell over her shoulders, tangled and wild. Like she'd been through a rainstorm and wildly fucked. My shirt hung long down her thighs, but knowing she was bare, what her breasts looked like beneath, had me going instantly hard.

She bit her lip, glanced around, up at the sky. Then at me. At my bare chest. I had on my jeans, nothing else.

"That you had to wait for me. I assume you want to get back."

I crooked my finger and she came down the two steps and onto the damp grass, her feet bare. From twenty feet away, I could see her hot pink toenails, her toned calves, the way her fingers nervously plucked at the hem of my shirt.

"While the weather's better, it's late. If we left now, we wouldn't return to the ranch until after dark. We'll spend the night here."

"Won't they be worried where we are?" she asked, biting her lip.

"I called the front desk, let them know we were here, that you were fine and also that the cabin was occupied."

She frowned. "You called?"

"There's no electric or water, but there's cell reception," I explained. "Matt and Ethan—the owners—have it so there's service anywhere on the Hawk's Landing property. All employees have phones with them for safety, but don't usually tell the guests about it."

"We're staying the night. Here. Together?" The last word came out as a squeak.

I cocked my head toward the cabin. "Micah and I can sleep outside if you want, but I have to admit, I'd rather be in that big bed with you. Between us."

"Oh," she murmured.

"You're blushing." After what we'd done, I was surprised I'd scandalized her.

She looked at the coiled rope in my hand, then at me.

"This isn't me. Really. I don't...I don't sleep around." She tossed her hands up. "God, I don't—didn't used to—sleep with strangers."

No, I didn't think she ever did. She wasn't a virgin, but she needed at least a connection with the man—or men—she gave herself to. Trust. "After what we did, I don't think we're strangers, do you?"

She cocked her hip and bent her knee, shifting her weight. My question made her blush even more. "I wanted some fun and it's over. You got what you wanted."

I heard the defensiveness in her tone. Reflex or avoidance of the truth? "If I couldn't see that you're embarrassed by what we did, I'd take offense to that."

"Well, you did," she countered, her hands going to her hips. "Got what you wanted, I mean." The move made my shirt ride up her thighs an inch or two. I saw her stance as more endearing than argumentative.

"And so did you, if I remember correctly. What was it, five times?" I could think of every single one of them.

She looked away, anywhere but at me.

"There's no reason to be embarrassed about what we did. What we made you feel."

"I'm not like that," she said, repeating her earlier words.

I nodded once. "I believe you. And that's one of the things that's so appealing about you. You've had some time to think and are wondering why you said yes to us."

"Yes," she agreed, dropping her hands, going over to the porch rail and wrapping her fingers around it. I ached to go to her, to bend her over that rail, watch my shirt ride up and then fuck her. Out in the open where her screams would echo off the mountains.

"To two men," I added. I was saying what she wouldn't, but I wanted to get all her worries out in the open. To address each one and put it behind us. Unless she was wildly open to threesomes— which I knew she wasn't since she'd admitted to never being with two men before—or she grew up in Bridgewater, this was going to be a struggle for her. This meaning being with both Micah and me. Permanently.

"Yes!" she said, her voice rising, her hands going up in the air.

I wanted to get closer to her, to pull her into my arms, but I worried she'd bolt. So I stood still, hands at my sides, coiled rope slack in my fingers.

"There's something between us, sugar. Can't you feel it?"

"We have chemistry." She shrugged as if what this was between us was just chemistry. Fuck no. It was so much more than that. "It's been awhile for me. I'm on vacation and this is a fling. You heard my sister on the damned speakerphone, I needed to get laid."

"I'll agree with the last. You did need to get laid."

Her lips thinned and I held up my free hand.

"But not just with any guy. Not some guy on your flight, not the rental car agent. Not even the guy at the reception desk. You wanted us. Why?" I paused, but answered for her. "Because you're drawn to us just as we're drawn to you."

"I don't even know you," she snapped.

"I could say I know what you look like

when you come or the color of your nipples. I know you have a scar on the inside of your knee and a little mole on the inside of your thigh. Just as well as you know the feel of my dick on your tongue."

Her cheeks flushed again, this time for a completely different reason.

"That's it, I'm out of here." She turned on her heel but before she could get up the two steps to the porch, I'd dropped the rope to the ground except for the tail end, circled it over my head and whipped my wrist, sending it through the air so the lasso wrapped around her. All the years competing in calf roping finally paid off.

As soon as it got about her waist, I tugged, tightening the loop, but not too hard to have her fall over.

She gasped, spun about, but her arms were pinned at her side. She wasn't as wiggly as a calf, but she was just as ornery about being roped. "Colt!"

I reeled her in, hand over hand on the rope as I walked toward her until she stood in front of me. "Let me go."

"Trying to get away?" Micah called, coming around the side of the cabin. Since we'd made the decision to spend the night, he'd been tending to the horses, settling them into the lean-to and small corral. He had one of the saddle bags which I knew held the food provided by the guest ranch kitchen for Lacey's outing. They never skimped— and had expected two guests, not one— so I had no doubt there was enough for us until we returned tomorrow. We wouldn't go hungry. If we got her soothed and settled, content to spend the night with us, my concern was whether we had enough condoms.

He set the bag on the porch, then joined me, putting his hand on her shoulder, sliding it down her arm.

"What's the matter?" he asked.

"Besides being hogtied?" She wriggled again, but the rope was snug about her elbows, securing them to her waist.

"That's not a hogtie. Trust me, sugar, those are no fun. This? This is just a way to keep you in one place so I can finish what I was saying."

She huffed and stomped her bare foot on the soft grass.

"What were you saying?" Micah asked.

"That while I didn't know everything about her, I knew some."

"Like the way she likes dirty talk?"

Her cheeks turned red and Micah grinned at the sight.

"That, but I was about to say that I wanted to know everything about her. I wanted to spend the night learning more. Out of bed. Then, hopefully, in."

"Why? You got what you wanted," she countered, repeating herself. She stuck out her lower lip and blew her hair out of her face. Since she didn't have use of her hands, I reached out, tucked the curl back behind her ear for her.

"Not even close." Her eyes lifted to mine at the sharper tone. I'd reined her in physically, but it was time to take over. "We want everything from you."

She frowned, stilled. "Everything? What does that even mean? Like money?"

Micah shook his head, ignored her ridiculous comment about money. "We want you. Your body, your heart. Your soul." I'd never heard Micah say those words before. They were too important, too valuable to say to just anyone.

"What?" she asked, her voice filled with soft confusion.

"We'd never have fucked you if we weren't planning on making you ours," he continued.

"Hell, we made you ours the second we sunk into your sweet pussy."

"But—"

Micah covered her mouth with his finger first, long enough to keep her quiet until he kissed her.

I watched as her body went from taut to languid and while the rope held her in place, Micah's hands on her arms kept her from falling to the ground.

"We're Bridgewater men, Lacey," Micah said. "Do you know what that means?"

A deep V formed in her brow. "That you grew up here. You told me that earlier."

"True," I said. "But in Bridgewater, it's common for two men to marry one woman."

Her mouth fell open and I saw her straight, white teeth. "That's insane."

"Nope. That's Bridgewater. The original founders back in the late 1800's followed a custom from a country called Mohamir. Heard they were stationed there in the British army. It's not around anymore, but their ways stuck. Two men—"

"Sometimes three," Micah added.

"—marry one woman. And it's usually love at first sight."

"Love—"

"Shh," Micah said, putting a finger over her lips. "We'll save that word for when the time's right. For now, just know we knew the second we saw you. You're the one for us."

"Most men in Bridgewater share a woman?" she asked.

"Matt and Ethan, Hawk's Landing's owners are engaged to Rachel. Having a baby together, even."

She stared at my chest and I could tell she was thinking, not ogling. "I met Matt when I arrived, but it wasn't as if he wore a sign saying he shared a fiancée."

I huffed out a small laugh.

"I told you I work with a chopper company that takes some of my clients into the backcountry," Micah said. "It's run by Rory and Cooper. They just married Ivy, their high school sweetheart."

"You want to marry me?" she asked, only after Micah kissed her once again. Her eyes were no longer narrowed, but a tad blurry. She seemed to like Micah's attentions.

"Not today," I replied, stroking a knuckle over her cheek. So damn soft. "Today we're going to get to know each other. So, no running off. This cabin is ours tonight. No one else is around. No distractions."

"Are you hungry?" Micah asked, stepping away and picking up the bag again. He walked up the steps, settled in one of the Adirondack chairs, began taking the food out and placing it on the small table.

"Yes, but I seem to be tied up at the moment," she grumbled, trying to get free of the rope, then glancing up at me. "Will you let me go?"

I walked around her once, circling more rope about her. "Nope. You're staying just like that."

"I can't feed myself with my arms pinned!"

I scooped her up in my arms honeymoon-style, and careful of the extra rope, walked up onto the porch and settled in the empty chair, Lacey in my lap. She wiggled and there was no doubt she could feel my hard cock.

When she stilled and her wide eyes turned to mine, I grinned. Yeah, she'd felt it all right.

"We'll feed you as we talk," Micah said.

The meal included slices of salami

and ham, a block of hard cheddar, olives, mixed nuts, a loaf of French bread, chocolate chip cookies and a thermos of iced tea. I knew there was more, but Micah had selected finger foods, easy to feed to our little captive.

Micah held up an olive. "Like these?"

She nodded and he put it to her lips. She took it, licking his fingers as she did.

Micah growled and I saw a gleam in Lacey's eyes.

"So, sugar. Tell us about yourself."

9

 ACEY

"I can't believe you want to marry me," I said, after swallowing the tangy olive. I was hungry. I'd certainly worked up an appetite. I hadn't eaten since lunch and not only did I have a three-hour trail ride, but a three-hour sex marathon, too.

Marry. They were insane. They were gorgeous, dominant and very alpha and yet they wanted to marry me? What man said that? They'd gotten what they wanted. Well fucked. All they had to do was take me back to my cabin at Hawk's Landing and I'd have a fling to remember for the foreseeable future. But no.

They seemed to want a relationship. A serious relationship with the end goal as marriage. Wow.

"Like I said, not today. That's a big deal and built on trust, friendship. So much," Colt said, grabbing a chunk of cheese that Micah had sliced. Nibbled. "You mentioned jet lag. I thought you came from LA."

I shifted my arms, tried to get my hands free of the soft rope. It was snug, but I still had feeling. "Can't you let me go?"

"Nope," Colt said, grinning. "You look good in my rope. Might have to try it again later. Ever been tied to a bed and fucked?"

My mouth fell open at the thought. My pussy, already a little achy from their thorough attentions earlier, seemed to like their ardent focus now, too. I'd never been tied up before, never really played much. It had just been sex, nothing too wild or adventurous. Definitely never five orgasms. Micah fed me a piece of cheese, then poured iced tea into a small plastic cup. He held it up for me, but I shook my head.

"Um...no."

Micah took a sip himself, put the cup down. "Colt's the champion with rope."

"You competed? Tying up women?"

Colt laughed and I loved the sound. Where Micah had on all of his clothes, Colt was shirtless—since I was wearing it—and the view was, well, spectacular. Sitting on the lap of a hot cowboy, one who was a gentle giant, felt good. He was warm, so very warm, like a furnace. I could only imagine snuggling up to him in bed on a cold winter night. Who needed a blanket?

The storm had blown off while I slept and the sky was clear. The air smelled damp, fresh. And Colt's shirt smelled like pure male. I had no doubt it was coated in pheromones making me all wild and lusty.

"You're the first woman I've ever roped. And, hopefully, the last." He curled a slice of salami and put it to my lips. I bit half of it and he fed himself the rest.

Neither of them wanted anything from me. No, they probably wanted my body again, but I knew they wouldn't just be using me. Not with five orgasms on my tally and only one each for them.

"You mentioned jet lag, sugar," he prompted again.

He'd been listening.

"I was in Korea. I got back the other day to LA, but had to get out of town."

"Did something happen?" Micah asked, his gaze sharpening.

I shrugged, glanced out at the lake. They were being honest with me, perhaps too honest, and I felt compelled to do the same. "There was a guy. Everyone thought we were dating, but it wasn't really true." Micah fed me a salted almond. "I came home to a crazy party at my house with him in my bed fucking a blonde."

Both men's bodies stiffened as if they were ready to go to LA and beat Chris up.

"You broke up two days ago?" Micah asked.

I shook my head, making sure they understood. "It happened the other day, yes. But we weren't really dating, so I wouldn't say we broke up."

"Your sister said you needed to get laid. What are we, rebound guys?"

I narrowed my eyes. Anger pumped through me hot and swift and it made me clench my hands into fists. "You were eager to hop into bed with me without knowing this. Why are you upset now?" I asked Colt.

"We don't care about your past, who you've been with. We only care about your future," Micah said.

"When we kissed you earlier, those were your last first kisses, sugar." Colt seemed very adamant. While he knew first hand I wasn't a virgin, he seemed to really wish there had been no previous guys in my life.

"You're so sure of this," I countered, studying his rugged face. I wanted to reach up, stroke his jaw and feel the rasp of his whiskers.

Colt grinned wickedly and it made

my nipples harden. He was so damned confident. "Yes, ma'am."

I sighed. Clarified. "You aren't rebound guys. I never slept with Chris. Everyone thought we had, that we were getting married even. But it was all lies. I don't even like him." I pursed my lips. "He's an asshole who fucked a random woman in my bed. In my house. I don't stand for that. Maybe you do since you shared me."

Colt's eyes narrowed and he tipped my chin up with his fingers. "Micah and I don't share you. You're ours. As for other guys? Not happening. We might be a threesome, but all we want is you."

Oh. That was pretty darn clear.

"You said everyone thought you were together with this guy. Who's everyone? Your parents?" Micah asked.

My father had been out of the picture since I was four. Divorced and moved to

Alabama to be with his secretary. As for my mother, she knew the deal. Knew I wouldn't stand for the stuff Chris did, nor anything the tabloids wrote. She'd raised me well enough to not be a doormat to any man. "No, the media. Well, the tabloids."

"Tabloids? Why the hell are tabloids keeping track of you?" Micah asked.

"I told you I'm an actress. I'm in a show on TV and the tabloids like to print stuff about me."

"You were in Korea for work?"

I nodded. "I have a big following over there. The show does."

Both were quiet as they absorbed my words.

"What about you?" I asked Colt. "You're a champion roper. What else?"

He grabbed a few olives, popped them in his mouth. "I told you I have my own ranch. It's a thirty-acre spread in the prettiest valley you'll ever see."

I had to wonder about that since

where we were right now was amazing. I could only imagine what his property looked like.

"I live in a small cabin on the property, and I'll build a house and stables over time. Until then, I'm foreman for Ethan and Matt."

"And you?" I glanced at Micah.

"I went to college for business, then came back here. I like the wide-open spaces and sharing it with others. An adventure company seemed like a good fit. So far, it's been going well."

"You're a full-service company," I commented, thinking of how well they were taking care of me—with and without my clothes.

He smiled, ran a finger down my nose. "Just for you. And remember, we canceled your trip, so you're not really a client."

"Had enough?" Colt asked.

"Food?"

"What else did you have in mind?" he asked.

I raised my eyebrows. This was where I got to decide how the rest of the night went. I could tell them no, that I wasn't interested and they'd back off. Even sleep outside. But we'd all know it was a lie. How I'd responded to them earlier couldn't have been faked. I wasn't that good of an actress.

Did I take them at their word, that they were interested in more with me? That this wasn't just a quick vacation fling? It wasn't as if I mentioned more to them and they were stringing me along. They'd brought it up. I was a sure thing. They could have just said we'd all have fun in this remote cabin and then part ways, well satisfied, back at Hawk's Landing.

But they hadn't. In fact, they really did seem to want more. But then again, so had Chris. And I'd been burned in the past by those spouting whatever they thought I wanted to hear to get something from me. But now? I was sitting in one guy's lap while another fed me. They were eager for more sex. And they'd give it to me, I just had to say the word.

I'd panicked when I'd woken up, my body sated and a little sore from their attentions. It so wasn't like me. But I'd done it and I'd enjoyed it. They'd been attentive and kind, wild and very sexy. Playful even. What woman in their right mind denied herself more?

Not me. Whatever tomorrow brought, it didn't matter right now. No one knew I was at Hawk's Landing. No one knew I was in this remote cabin. I could be myself. No acting. No pretense.

For once, I could be Lacey Leesworth and take two cowboys for another ride as if I were a rodeo queen. None of the things the tabloids said about me had been true. But I wanted to do something as wild and crazy as what they'd come up with and actually be fact. For once.

"Lacey?" Colt prompted.

I angled my head down, glanced at Micah through my lashes. "I'm the one that's tied up." If the look didn't give them ideas, the tone of my voice had to.

"You're at our mercy then?" Micah asked, one pale brow arched.

I bit my lip. Nodded.

"We need to hear you say it, sugar. Tell us what you want."

I glanced between them. "You." Heat flared in their gazes and I felt Colt's cock pulse against my hip. "For tonight."

I wasn't saying I wanted more than that. I couldn't. Not yet. I felt more for these two men than I had any before. It was insane, this instant attraction. No, it was more than attraction. I really wanted to get to know them, to be with them. I felt safe. I felt desired. Cherished. And not because I was Lacey Lee. They didn't seem to care that I was famous or that I had more money than I ever imagined. They just wanted to feed me olives and fuck me.

I was fine with that.

"We'll start with tonight," Colt replied. Clearly, he wanted more but would settle for this. For now. Come tomorrow, I imagined them to be very persuasive again. And if by persuasive they were hot and attentive lovers, then I didn't stand much of a chance.

10

 ACEY

Colt wrapped an arm about my waist, picked me up and carried me over to the porch railing, bending me over it. He knelt on the plank floor and tugged on the rope, ensuring the lasso was still about my waist, but the rest of the rope he took and tied off on the bottom rail. Not only were my arms pinned at my sides, but I was now very securely tied to the railing.

Micah had stepped down from the porch and came to stand in front of me. He only had to bend at the waist a little so we were eye-to-eye. "Not too tight?" he asked.

I shook my head.

"Can you wiggle your fingers?"

I tried and I could. They weren't numb. Colt tucked his beneath the edge of the rope about my waist, my wrists, checking it.

"Okay, sugar?" he asked. He'd stood and leaned over me. I felt the heat of his chest against my back, even through the soft fabric of his shirt.

I was secure—I wasn't going anywhere—but not uncomfortable. "Yes."

"You still want to be at our mercy?" he asked, kissed my neck, tugged at the collar of the shirt and laved my shoulder.

One of the snaps came undone, gave him a few inches more access. Micah reached beneath me, tugged on the shirt a little more so the fabric parted and my breasts were exposed, yet keeping the material between my lower belly and the wood railing.

I felt the tail of Colt's shirt flip up over my back just before his hand came down on my bottom. I startled at the hot sting of his palm. "Micah asked you a question, sugar." His tenderness of his voice contradicted the action.

"Yes, I still want to be at your mercy."

They could see all of me; my breasts were exposed to the cool air and I knew there had to be a pink handprint on my right butt cheek. Not only that, but from his position on the porch, Colt couldn't miss every wet inch of my pussy. I was bent over and completely open. Completely vulnerable.

I wasn't sure how Colt sensed it,

but his next words eased me. "All I have to do is tug on the knot on the rail and you'll be free. Just say the word, sugar and we'll let you go. Don't be afraid."

"That's right," Micah added. "Give in and enjoy. See how two men can pleasure you when all you have to do is feel. We might push you a bit—I can tell you haven't been spanked before, but you like it. I promise you're going to come."

I gasped when Colt cupped my pussy, felt how wet and eager I was. "She likes being tied up. Knowing there's nothing she can do but take whatever we give her."

He slipped a finger inside me and I groaned. He spanked me again and I clenched down on the single digit. Whimpered. Colt swore as he cupped my ass, soothed the heated area. "I'm going to come all over your pale skin if you keep making those sexy little sounds."

"You've never been tied up before. What else haven't you done?" Micah asked. He looked me in the eye, his gaze heated, yet filled with something like amusement. "Fucked from behind?" He studied me. "Hmm. Two men at the same time?"

I flushed, even though I was already bent over a porch railing and completely exposed. "I thought that's what we did earlier."

He grinned. "You mean sucking Colt's cock as I fucked you?"

I nodded, my hair falling down past my shoulders. He brushed it back for me. "That's one way to take the two of us. What about having one cock in your pussy, the other in your ass?"

Colt's finger began to move in and out, slowly fucking me. Like really, really slowly, which was revving my engine and pissing me off a bit at the same time. It was also making my brain stall.

In my—? My mouth fell open. Oh yeah, the lube conversation. I was not going to ask my sister after her knowledge of the necessity of lube, nor was I going to tell her any of the ways these guys intended to use it.

"Um...I told you I haven't been with two guys before."

"Then you've never played here before?" Colt slipped his finger from my pussy, slid it up and over my back entrance. I cried out and my eyes widened as he touched that very intimate place. Micah was watching me closely and I saw the way his pale eyes darkened at my awakened awareness.

It didn't hurt. In fact, Colt was barely touching me. It actually felt really good. But I clenched down instinctively, which only made me feel empty and want to be fucked. I ached for their big cocks. Not in my ass —no way.

"Did you pack the lube your sister mentioned?" Colt asked, continuing to circle his finger, the motion easy since it was slick with my arousal.

I closed my eyes, bit my lip as Colt used his other hand—I imagined it was his other hand as I had no idea how he'd be so dexterous otherwise—to find my clit and begin to play.

"Did you?" Micah repeated, brushing a knuckle over my nipple.

I nodded and I gasped at the feel. My breath came out in pants as if I were running a sprint instead of remaining completely still. I didn't know where to concentrate. My nipples tightened from the slight touch, my clit swelled, my pussy felt completely ignored and my ass, well, it had nerve endings sparking and firing. I was going to come.

I wiggled my hips and shifted my feet

—the only thing I could do tied up as I was. My fingers clenched into fists at my sides. "I'm going to—oh god!"

I came. Hard. Like ridiculously hard since they weren't doing much more than caressing me. In very specific places.

I cried out. There was no way I could keep the sounds in, the only outlet I had for the release to escape.

"Good girl," Micah crooned in my ear, kissing the outer swirl, then along my cheek. I lifted my head so we could kiss. I instantly opened my mouth, finding his tongue with mine. I needed more, voracious and eager.

I felt a little tug, then the release of the rope. "You've been tied up long enough, sugar." Colt's big hands stroked up and down my arms and he took my hands, placed them on the railing. "That doesn't mean we want you to move. Stay right there," he warned. I guessed he'd spank me again if I didn't comply.

I was too hot, too eager for them to argue and so I remained bent over the railing. Micah moved away and I heard his footfall on the steps and into the cabin. He returned quickly and I heard the sound of a plastic flip top just before I felt the cold drizzle of the lube.

"You won't fit," I said, coming up some and looking over my shoulder. Colt put a hand on the center of my back and gently pushed me back down.

With his other hand, he began to play with my ass hole again, working the lube in. Squirting more, then pressing against my untried hole. "No cocks here tonight, sugar. We'll just play. Prepare you for when we do take you. You're going to love it. Then, and now."

I had a deliciously dark feeling he was right. They hadn't done anything I hadn't loved so far, but it was hard to think about his words—when we do take you—because that meant they really did want longer than just tonight. I was only in Montana for the week, then I'd be returning to LA, to the cluster that was my life. To whatever the latest lies the tabloids were spreading.

"Whoa, sugar. Where'd you go just then?"

"What?" I asked.

Colt gave my ass a playful swat. "Your mind went somewhere. Am I losing my touch?"

I had to laugh and was impressed he'd somehow noticed. I had to wonder if he were a mind reader, although I must have tightened my fingers on the railing or something. His touch was on my clit and ass. When he pressed his finger a touch harder, my resistant muscle gave way and he slipped into me to the knuckle. Slick and hard, he barely

breached my ass. That was enough.
Whoa.

"Nope. I'm back. Right here. Oh..."

"Good girl," Colt said.

I heard the sound of a condom
wrapper, then the slide of a zipper. "Colt
got you all ready for me?"

Turning my head, I saw that Micah
had stripped off his shirt and opened his
jeans, his hard cock sheathed and ready
for me. The hair on his head was darker
—as if it had been bleached by all the
time in the sun—than the smattering on
his chest,

Oh, yes. I was ready for him. All I
could do was nod as Colt moved away
and Micah stepped behind me. I felt the
nudge of his cock at my entrance, the
cool drip of more lube. "Ready?"

His cock pressed in and so did his
thumb on my ass. I dropped my head to
my hands, nodded.

My head came up and I arched my

back when he filled me. Both holes. Carefully, but insistently. No one had ever done this to me before.

My pussy was so wet, I could hear the sound of it. But Micah's thumb? Holy hell. I'd never felt so full. A hand gripped my hip and he began to move. My breasts swayed and I pressed back, wanting more.

"Like that, do you? Imagine what it will be like with a cock in your ass instead of my thumb," Micah said. His voice was a growl and I knew he was struggling to even talk.

"It's so good. I never knew," I breathed, my fingers white on the railing. "More."

This wasn't sweet or tame. No, it was wild. Uninhibited. So completely, totally unlike me. Or what I thought was me. Until now.

Now, something in me cracked open and I didn't think I could ever go back.

The slaps of Micah's hips against my butt came faster. Harder.

Colt knelt, leaned against the railing, reached up and brushed my clit.

"Now, sugar."

Yeah, that was all it took. Just the slightest brush of his finger.

Perspiration dotted my skin as I clenched and squeezed down on Micah's cock and thumb. They didn't stop moving, in and out, as I came.

"Too much. Too good," Micah growled, then held himself deep. His fingers would leave bruises on my hip, I was sure, but I didn't care.

They wanted me, so much that they lost their heads. Knowing I did that to them was powerful. Heady.

"I don't think I'm ever going to get enough," Micah breathed as he carefully pulled out.

I stood, felt used and sated, relaxed

and I couldn't help the grin that spread across my face.

"What's that look for, sugar?" Colt asked.

I glanced up, studied him. From his almost-black gaze to his clenched jaw, broad shoulders and down to the hard cock behind his jeans. "You. It's all for you."

I wasn't done. I was just getting started. These two made me insatiable. If I liked—no, loved—ass play, then there had to be more to discover. And with these two, they made it easy, risk-free to have fun and explore. Discover myself and what this was between us.

"You had your way, cowboy. Now it's my turn." I didn't know where the saucy tone came from, and the grin on Colt's face said he liked it.

Micah had gone inside, most likely to dispose of the condom, and Colt and I were alone.

"You want to be in charge?" he asked, cocking a brow.

"I do." I pushed on his chest and he stepped back. If he hadn't wanted to, there was no way I'd be able to move him. He was too big. Too strong.

He settled back into the Adirondack chair with one final push, his hands settling on the wide armrests. I climbed onto his lap, straddled his hips. Glancing up at him through my lashes, I said, "I learned to ride a horse. Think I can ride a cowboy?"

My fingers fumbled with the button and zipper on his jeans and quickly discovered that was all he was wearing. His cock all but fell into my hands. Micah came back out. He dropped a condom onto the armrest, then moved to lean against the rail, his long legs stretched out. With his hands on the railing on either side of him, he settled in to watch.

"Put it on," Colt said, angling his head to the condom.

With an eagerness that surprised me, I worked the condom on his hard cock, then shifted up onto my knees. Colt's shirt only had a few buttons at the bottom holding it together, but my breasts were still exposed. It was almost like peekaboo and seemed a touch more erotic; wearing the shirt of the guy I was about to fuck was totally hot.

Colt didn't touch me, just pressed his head back into the chair and watched. His cock was so big, it was easy to have him slide over my pussy, then settle at my entrance. I met his gaze, held it as I lowered myself, began to ride him.

His jaw tightened as I circled my hips, began to move faster. He leaned forward, latched onto a nipple suckled. My inner muscles clenched down as he did so.

This new angle, it took him so deep,

offering a slight bite of pain, just shy of uncomfortable.

"This, sugar," Colt said, his breath fanning my wet tip. "This is special. What we have, fuck, it's so good."

"Yes," I agreed. It was almost too good.

I was going to come again, my clit rubbing against him every time I took him deep.

"You're ours, Lacey." Micah's words came from behind me, but I was too lost in my pleasure to process them.

Colt's hands finally came to my hips, helped me ride him until we came, our shouts mingled, until I slumped down onto his hard chest, heard the frantic beat of his heart. Knew it matched mine.

This might have been a sex-fest, but Colt was right. This was special. I just didn't know what to do about it.

$\mathcal{M}$ICAH

"This is it then," Lacey said after I helped her down from her horse. We were in front of her cabin back at Hawk's Landing and she was fidgeting and looking anywhere but at us. It was almost noon; she'd slept part of the morning away. I was used to getting up early, but I hadn't minded lying in bed, watching her sleep. It was only when she stirred that we claimed her again. Yes, claimed.

She might not have felt that way about what we did, but there was no question for me. Where we'd been playful and wild the night before, we were gentle with her, slow, coaxing orgasm after orgasm from her before I carried her out to the lake.

Because of this, her words were like a blow. She thought we were through.

"It?" I asked, glancing at Colt. His gaze was in shadow from his hat, but I could see the way his jaw tightened. He wasn't pleased she could let what we shared go so easily.

Or was it a defense mechanism? Was she saying it was over first, just to keep from having us do it? We had no intention of it, and it was our job to set her straight.

"Our fling."

"Fling?" Colt asked, stepping up to

her, taking her chin and tipping her head up so she had to look at both of us. We stood before her. Close, but not too close. While those in Bridgewater were fine about a threesome, the Hawk's Landing guests weren't from the area. Like Lacey, they didn't know about our ways. While no one was ashamed of their relationships, no one flaunted it either. I wasn't ashamed of what I felt for Lacey, what I would share with my best friend, but it was obvious Lacey wasn't there yet.

"This isn't a fling, sugar. Go get cleaned up and we'll be back in an hour to take you to lunch. I think there's a barbecue on the south field."

"Wait." She held up her hand. "You're serious, aren't you?"

"About barbecue? Hell, yes. The cook's famous for his brisket."

She rolled her eyes. "Not barbecue. Us."

"Have we once said otherwise?" I asked. "We're serious as two men can be."

She shook her head. "But...it's one thing for us to be together in a mountain cabin—"

"And on the porch," Colt cut in to say.

"And the lake," I added, my cock getting hard. "I kept you warm as I fucked you in that clear water."

I grinned at her pretty flush. Yeah, it had been that good. She'd had her legs wrapped around my waist as I filled her. The water had been mountain run-off cold, but I'd kept her warm. I'd seen Colt leaning on the porch railing, watching.

"That's just it. I can't...can't do that with you here. There are people around." She glanced left and right, but couldn't see much past us. We were blocking her view of the rest of the ranch, although there wasn't much to see, her cabin set far away from all the others. It was perfect for a honeymoon, or for two men interested in a certain lady.

"We're gentlemen," I reminded her as I placed a hand on her shoulder. She wore the same clothes as the day before, not Colt's shirt. She was perfect as-is, especially since I knew she was all dirty from Colt and I touching her. "What we do with you is private. Just between us. We're not going to toss you over the buffet table and have our way with you."

Colt glanced at me, tipped his hat back on his forehead. "No, we'll do that later. After the picnic, we'll take you to my ranch. I want you to see it."

He'd talked about it on our ride back, sharing his schedule for finishing up the main house, the stable, his plans for training horses—and the idea to move the base of my business there. She'd been interested, clearly seeing this was a passion of his. She was a career woman, had her own dreams and passions and was following through with them. Understood that it was crucial to having a fulfilling life.

She looked between us, debating. Colt wouldn't let go of her chin until she made a decision. The right decision, which was "Yes."

"All right."

"One hour, Lacey," I said.

"If you're late, we'll take you into your cabin and spank that sweet ass of yours before we go."

We left her there, her mouth hanging open and her cheeks flushed even hotter as we led the horses toward the stables.

———

Lacey

. . .

I pulled the phone away from my ear as my sister screamed. "Oh my god. Oh my god. Oh my god!"

I rolled my eyes.

"Stop!" I groaned.

"I will...I promise. Oh my god."

She'd been saying that over and over for the past minute. I'd called to tell her everything. Well, almost everything. I couldn't keep it to myself. It was too crazy. Too overwhelming.

"Were they good?" Before I could reply, she prattled on. "Of course, they were good. I bet they had cock monsters, didn't they?"

I thought of Micah and Colt, and their cocks. Yes, they fell under the classification of monster sized.

"Okay, give me the details. Every one of them."

I sat down on the edge of my bed. This cabin was rustic but had more amenities than the one in the backcountry. The one I'd probably remember for the rest of my life. Having a bathroom—a toilet and shower—were definite perks. But I was all alone. Somehow, I missed Colt and Micah. It had been ten minutes since they'd sauntered off to the stable and I'd been able to ogle their perfect cowboy backsides.

"There was a thunderstorm," she supplied. "Start there. Don't leave anything out."

I had to laugh. For once, Ann Marie was living vicariously through me. Years ago, she'd been a little star struck by my job, by the fame. But she'd quickly learned that being a star wasn't all it was cracked up to be and began to empathize with my very sheltered—and completely exposed—life. And she'd married Mr. Perfect. Tall, dark, handsome...and rich. Gabe was everything a woman wanted, not that

Ann Marie was a gold digger. But he was actually madly in love with my sister and that was all that mattered. I'd give up my career and fortune for true love like hers.

Now it was her turn to be envious.

"I have less than an hour to get ready before they come back."

"They're coming back?" She squealed again. "Lacey, does that mean they want more? It wasn't just a one-night-stand?"

"They want forever."

That shut her up. The line was completely silent and I pulled the phone away from my head again to make sure the connection hadn't dropped.

"I'm sorry, what? Forever? As in... long term?"

"I'm pretty sure that's what forever means," I said. I plucked at the pretty quilt on the bed.

"Yeah, but...you just met them! And I

put the emphasis on them. Did you even have time to talk?"

I couldn't help but grin, even though she couldn't see it. "Yes, we talked. And as for the them thing, Bridgewater accepts plural marriages."

"Marriage? You mean they want to marry you? Lacey, either you were incredible in bed or these men...what? Had love at first sight?"

I felt a smidge hurt by her words, that I wasn't worth a lifetime commitment.

"I didn't mean it like that," she plowed on as if sensing my feelings. "Not about your mad sex skills, which I'm sure they're fantastic, but of course they'd fall in love with you right away. You're fabulous and if they see that in you, then I like them."

I thought of Micah, his easygoing demeanor, his quick smile. Then Colt, with his intense bearing, yet gentle touch. Was it possible it was love at first sight?

"They never used the "L" word," I told her. "But no guy uses the "F" word either if they don't mean it."

"They don't swear?"

It felt good to laugh. "No, not that "F" word. I meant forever. No guy would say they wanted forever if they didn't mean it. I mean, if they wanted to keep having sex with me, they could have said we'd have fun the rest of my vacation. A clear end date. But no. They didn't give themselves that out."

"Wow."

"I was the one who'd said I only wanted one night."

"You did?" she asked. "Hang on." I heard her hand go over the phone, her voice muffled for a minute. "Gabe says he wants to meet them. Do not marry them until he does a background check on them."

I stood, went to the window and looked out at the creek. It was running a little higher than it had the day before, but the storm had dropped a lot of rain.

"He's the one who eloped with you," I reminded her. "He might run a high-tech company, but he is not looking into Colt and Micah."

"Colt and Micah," she repeated, but I knew she was telling Gabe. "She hasn't said her last names. No, she'll kill me. Yes, they work for the guest ranch."

"Ann Marie," I groaned.

"Let him do his thing. He's your brother now and is protective of you, too," she countered, then whispered. "Good, he's gone off to play golf. Now tell me about the sex."

Talking to her was like a bad case of whiplash.

"Amazing."

"I tell you about my sex life," she grumbled when I didn't say more.

"No, you don't. And please, don't start now." I loved Gabe, but I didn't want to know about what he and my sister did together. It was one thing when we were younger and dated a bunch of different guys, but I had to get together with Gabe for the rest of my life.

"Fine. But you have to at least tell me what it's like being with two guys at once. It's not every day a woman gets two cowboys."

I went into the bathroom, stood before the sink and looked at myself in the mirror. I was a little bedraggled, my hair a wild tangle. First, it had gotten wet in the storm, then it dried while I'd napped, then a night of sex, then a sexy dip in the lake. My on-set hairstylist would keel over, but I had to grin. I had I've-just-been-well-fucked hair.

"I didn't have two at once," I admitted.

"You mean—" She cleared her throat. "You didn't use the lube?"

I remembered being bent over the porch railing, the drizzle of lube and the play of Colt's fingers. Micah's thumb as he fucked me.

"We used the lube, but not for what you're thinking. At least not yet. They said I needed to be prepared first. It was just play."

"Oh my god." She said it a few more times. We were back to that again. I sighed, but it felt good for her to be okay with what I'd done. I shouldn't need validation, but a girl needed her sister sometimes.

"You know what this means?" she asked, once she pulled herself together.

"That I've got anal sex in my future?"

"That, but it means forever."

I sat down on the lip of the claw foot tub. "How does lube mean forever? They could just want to double team me and put notches in their headboards."

"True, but not with these two. They're not players. They're honest-to-God, real life, honorable cowboys."

"Who like to fuck," I added. "A lot."

"Even better. You've told me what they want. How do you feel about them?"

I stood, tucked the phone between my cheek and my shoulder and worked off my socks and jeans. I had to multi-task here if I was going to be ready for Micah and Colt in the hour window they'd given me. The idea of a spanking had my nipples hardening, but I needed a breather. I was a little sore. It was their intensity, though, that had me wanting a little break from sexy times. I had to figure out what I wanted from them. Ann Marie's question was timely.

How did I feel about them?

"I don't know very much about them.

193

Micah runs an outdoor adventure company and Colt, while he works here at Hawk's Landing, has land he wants to turn into his own ranch."

"Family?"

"You mean are they married?" I asked.

She sighed. "No. I mean, parents, siblings."

"One set lives here, the other moved to Arizona. Still married, from what they've said."

"So they have jobs, don't live in their parents' basements. They kept you safe in a dangerous storm and kept you very warm last night."

"I don't know if they have food allergies or if they leave the seat up on the toilet. I have no idea if they have a gambling addiction or if one of them has a houseful of parakeets."

"Parakeets?"

"You know what I mean. I know nothing about them."

"While I knew Gabe didn't have any tropical birds in his house, I wasn't aware he drank OJ out of the carton until we were engaged and I hadn't even realized he shaved his balls until I walked in on him in the shower two days ago."

I was lifting my shirt over my head when she said the last and I stopped, horrifically imagining Gabe shaving his balls, and I got tangled.

When I put the phone back to my ear, I had to yell. "Ann Marie, I told you. TMI!"

"Sorry, but you get the idea."

"I got the idea without knowing about Gabe's balls."

"So how do you feel about them? Your cowboys, not Gabe's balls."

I glanced down, saw the hickey on the upper swell of my right breast. I didn't remember when I got it exactly, but I did remember the very serious, very thorough attention Micah gave my breasts.

"I like them. They like me. The real me. They know what I do, I told them, but they know nothing about the show and didn't seem to care I was famous."

"Honey, from what it sounds like, you could have told them you were a parakeet breeder and they wouldn't have minded."

"That's my point. They want to be with me. It was the first time in...well, forever, that I didn't have to be "on." I didn't have to pretend or act. And they're nothing like the guys I know in LA. They're real. Honest. It's...easy."

"That's when you know it's the real thing."

"What? Easy?"

"Yes. It just is." Her voice had changed from squealing madwoman to tender-hearted sister. "Now what?"

"Now I hustle to take a shower and go to a barbecue with them."

"Okay, I'll let you go, but I want to hear more about this Bridgewater thing. I'll have Gabe look into it."

I groaned, then laughed. "I'll talk to you later."

"Have fun—use condoms!"

I hung up, tossed my phone on the bed, smiling. I couldn't help it. I had two men who were interested in me. Not just one. Two. It felt really good. Not love good, but amazing. I would go with it. See where this thing went. Worst case, I'd be leaving in a few days with an amazing fling to remember. Best case... well, that was still undecided.

12

$\mathcal{M}$ICAH

"You're Jane Goodheart!"

"Oh my goooooood, I've been in love with you ever since that evil man, Ramos, bit you and made you a vampire. Where's Kade?"

We'd handed off the horses to the guys working in the stable and took showers in the employee locker room before collecting Lacey from her cabin.

Had we known she was to be accosted at the outdoor lunch, we would have avoided it entirely.

But we'd had no idea how famous she really was.

When we'd knocked on her door, she'd been ready, dressed in a pretty sundress. It was modestly cut, but I couldn't miss her delectable curves. My cock got hard at the sight of her, knowing exactly what was beneath, but since it was demure, it ensured no one else would.

"Is this okay?" she'd asked, glancing down at her outfit.

"For the picnic? Yes. To keep our hands off you? It's going to be hard," Colt said, shifting his cock in his clean jeans.

"That's not the only thing," she replied, grinning.

Colt cupped her waist, pulled her in for a kiss. He rolled his hips and I knew she felt him. "Damn straight. Are you sure we can't stay here and have a picnic of our own?" Colt leaned in, murmured in her ear. "We'd take turns eating you."

Lacey licked her lips and I saw the heat in her eyes. She knew we'd follow through on his words if she said yes. "Oh no. I want some of this barbecue. I've worked up an appetite." She squeezed between us and down the steps as if she had to get as far away from a bed—and privacy—as possible to ensure we didn't get between her thighs.

We'd made it through the buffet line and had our hands full with loaded plates of smoked meat, side salads and sliced fruit, cutlery and drinks. But a couple blocked our way to one of the picnic tables spread out across the flat area behind the main lodge, stopping us. Or at least stopping Lacey.

They were in their thirties, with big smiles and eager gazes. The man wore jeans and a pale blue golf shirt with sneakers. The woman wore a black skirt and white tank top with cowboy boots. Based on their Southern accents, I had to assume her footwear was brand new.

The wife, who had to be five feet tall, pushed Colt out of the way, his lemonade sloshing over the edge of his cup and dripped down his hand. Lacey backed up a step, bumping into me. Her ponytail brushed across my plate before I could move it out of the way and she had potato salad on the ends.

"Oh um...thanks," Lacey murmured. For a second, when the guy said she'd been bit and turned into a vampire, my mind had stalled. I thought the guy was insane. Her name wasn't Jane Goodheart. They must have mistaken her for someone else, but then I remembered she'd said she starred in a TV show about vampires.

The couple, who had the biggest,

goofiest grins, looked around. "Where's Kade?"

Who the fuck was Kade? I watched as Colt put his food down on the nearest table, wiped his hand on a napkin and watched closely. I didn't think he'd tackle the couple to the ground since they were ranch guests, but they were in Lacey's face. Not only was she also a guest, but she was ours. If she needed protecting, even from this duo, Colt would step in. So would I, brisket be damned.

"Kade's not real. He's just a character on the show," Lacey told them.

Their expressions drooped as if they'd just been told there was no Santa Claus.

"Yes, but you're Jane! I understand if you're taking a vacation—isn't this place fabulous?—but Kade should be with you."

"I'm not really Jane," Lacey clarified.

The woman waved her hand as if she

didn't believe her. "What did you do to your hair? We almost didn't recognize you."

I wasn't an expert on women's hairstyles, but her hair looked fine to me. I didn't see any difference in it from an hour ago.

Lacey lifted her hand to the side of her head, ran it down her ponytail, frowned when she felt the bits of potato salad. The woman reached out with her napkin and wiped off the food, stared at it. "Oh my god! This was on Jane Goodheart. Will you autograph it? I'll be able to sell it on eBay for like, a hundred dollars!"

I put my food down and—figuratively and literally—stepped between the couple and Jane...Lacey. They were way over the top. Completely in Lacey's face. "Let's let her eat her meal," I said.

The couple wasn't having any of it.

"It's Jane, everyone!"

People were staring because of the scene the couple was making. I heard some murmurs about recognizing Lacey, but they didn't really seem to care. Some people recognized boundaries.

"If I sign something for you, will you let me eat my lunch?" Lacey asked. I could hear the touch of aggravation in her voice, but her expression was as sweet as pie. Yeah, she was a good actress.

I wasn't. Colt wasn't either by the thunderous look on his face.

"Sure, sure," the husband said, pulling a pen out of the camo fanny pack about his waist. "Here. Make it out to Sam and Belinda."

"No," Belinda countered, looking at Sam. "We should just have the autograph so we can sell it. It's not like there are other Sam and Belinda's out there."

They bickered back and forth and Lacey grabbed the napkin and the pen from their hands, moved to the closest table and signed her name, careful not to tear it. Then she grabbed her own napkin and did a second autograph.

She spun back. "Here. Have a great vacation."

The couple stopped arguing and looked at Lacey. Took the napkins and pen. "Oh, thank you!" They started talking about how they liked her hair blonde better than how it was now. Dark. Lacey just smiled, picked up her food and cup and walked away. Colt followed right behind, ensuring there weren't any other rabid fans among the ranch's guests. I lingered behind and watched as Belinda lifted her phone and took a few candid pictures. "Enough," I told her, blocking her view of Lacey.

It was, perhaps, the harsh tone of my voice or the way I loomed a foot over her that the glee dropped from her face and she lowered her phone.

"Here at Hawk's Landing, we don't stand for harassment of other guests. I think you've found she's been more than generous with her attentions on her vacation and it's time to let her get back to it."

"But she's a vampire! She shouldn't be out during the day."

The woman was completely bat-shit crazy.

"I'll be sure to tell her," I replied, leaving them behind as I worked my way over to Colt and Lacey. They'd settled at a far picnic table, alone. Lacey sat facing away from the rest of the barbecue, her view was solely of the open field and the mountains in the distance. Colt had his eye on the group of guests, ensuring she didn't have any more surprises.

I settled beside her, my thigh brushing against hers. Colt was watching her, not eating. His hat sat on the table beside his plate. Lacey was picking at her food with her fork.

I leaned in, breathed in her soft scent. "Are you okay?"

She nodded.

"When you said you were in a successful TV show, I hadn't really ever thought about the implications of that," I said.

She looked to me. Gone was the carefree look she had when we were at the backcountry cabin, or even ten minutes ago. "I have a lot of fans."

"Not happening, sugar," Colt said, not liking her diplomatic answer. "You're a good actress, all right, hiding your true feelings, but not with us."

"You want me to be upset, to cry, because I had my hair felt up while on vacation? You want me to yell at the couple for selling potato salad on a napkin because it touched my hair?" She grabbed her ponytail, pulled it around her shoulder so she could look at the end, make sure there wasn't any food left on it.

"That's better," Colt replied. "I love knowing how you feel, even if it's angry. You can shout and scream all you want when we take you to my spread. All right?"

She nodded.

"Let's eat and we'll get out of here."

She picked up her fork and tucked into her meal. Fortunately, no one else approached. I glanced over my shoulder and saw a staff member in the usual uniform of golf shirt and jeans standing between us and the other tables. He faced the guests and was acting as a shield, ready to keep any other crazies away. One of the barbecue workers must have called in the confrontation to the office.

"Do you have people approach you

like this all the time?" Colt asked. He cut a piece of brisket, speared it with his fork.

"Yes, all the time. I haven't been to the grocery store since I found a picture of me online buying melon. The caption said I was deciding what size boob job I wanted."

I glanced down at her breasts, a perfect handful hidden beneath her dress. They were all natural. Colt and I knew that for a fact. And they were gorgeous. Tear drop shaped, lush. They'd swayed beautifully when she'd been bent over the porch rail and fucked.

I was angry for her, for something that had happened when I hadn't even known her.

"And your hair?" Colt asked.

"It's been blonde since the start of the show four years ago. The character, Jane, has fair hair so I have to keep it that way. But when I found my sort-of ex-fiancé in my bed fucking, I kind of lost it. That's why I came here. To escape. I'm not even registered, my sister is. I took over her reservation. When I landed in Bozeman, I had the taxi driver take me to a drug store. I colored it after I arrived."

"Sort-of ex-fiancé?" I asked.

"I told you about him yesterday. He's a rock star and my PR people put us together. They put a spin on it that we were dating to drum up popularity."

Colt glanced past us before looking at Lacey. "It doesn't seem like you need to be any more popular."

She took a bite of meat, nodded. "True. It was more for Chris than me. He needed more attention and I was it."

"So they used you."

I shrugged. "That's the industry."

"To make you have a fiancé? That's pushing it."

"The media came up with that on

their own. We didn't date. Not really. Just
went out with some people as a group. I
don't even like him. I never really did."

I wasn't sure if I should feel angry or
sorry for her. "Why didn't you just say
no? Tell the truth and do your own
thing?"

"I was too busy with work to really
care. I don't pay attention to the tabloids.
My sister, Ann Marie, does, but I avoid it
since it's all speculation and innuendo."

"Send the media a note. Or a phone
call."

"They'll spin it," she replied. "Any
way to sell magazines." She sighed,
poked at her cornbread with her fork. "I
work fifteen hour days until the filming
is done. Then, once that's over, I do press
junkets. That's why I was in Asia. Instead
of writing that our relationship had
grown cold, they'd said we'd gotten
engaged. I was mad about that, but
finding Chris had thrown a party,

trashed my house and fucked a blonde, I'd had enough." She sounded more angry and bitter than sad, and that was a good thing. She'd been a doormat for her PR people. No, not a doormat. A pawn, and she'd let them. It didn't seem like she was going to let that happen any longer. I was glad of it, and if she needed help standing up to this asshole who used her so fucking badly, to anyone else, we'd have her back.

"That's why I'm here. To get away. To figure out what I want to do."

Colt grunted, took a ruthless bite of his corn on the cob.

"So you're no longer fake engaged?" I asked.

"I have no idea. I'm not going online and my sister didn't mention anything when I talked to her earlier. At a minimum, people are going to comment on my change of hair color."

"I can't picture you blonde," I said,

running my hand over her head, feeling the silky strands. I knew she was a natural brunette; the little landing strip above her pussy was a gorgeous dark shade.

"You haven't watched TV. Or seen the Internet, or stood in the grocery checkout line to see the difference. Or any of the other things said about me."

"That bad, huh?" Colt asked.

"That bad," she repeated, taking a bite of her baked beans.

"You'll stay with me," Colt said.

"Us," I corrected. "Either at my house in town or at Colt's cabin on his property. Nowhere else. Your cabin's not safe with those looney bins at the ranch."

"Matt and Ethan will ensure your privacy," Colt added. "But I'd feel better if we could watch out for you."

"You can't protect me all the time," she countered.

"Oh? Why not? That's our job now," I

added. She was ours and we protected our woman.

Her mouth fell open in obvious surprise.

"Don't you have to work?" she asked, glancing between the two of us. I expected her to ask after my not-so-subtle statement about our role in her life, but she avoided it. That was fine. For now. This wasn't the place to continue our talk about more with her.

"I don't," I told her. "My next group comes in next week."

"I'll make arrangements to take a few days off," Colt said. "I'm sure Matt and Ethan will want personal protection for the rest of your stay. Me."

"Us," I corrected, again.

She put her fork down, took a sip of her lemonade. "You really want to do that? I can just stay in my cabin and read."

No fucking way. I shook my head.

"That's not fair to you."

She laughed, but it wasn't because she was amused. "I learned that life isn't fair a long time ago. Rich and famous means my life's an open book. Remember, those people thought I was Jane. Not Lacey."

"You done?" I asked, glancing at her plate, then her. Her dark eyes met mine.

"Yes."

"Let's get out of here."

"Are you sure?" she asked.

Colt reached across the table, took her hand. "Sugar, we've been saying all along we want you. Only you. Come with us."

"Don't you dare say you thought it was a one-night-stand," I added, knowing that was going to come next.

She closed her mouth. Yeah, I'd been right on that.

"We want it all, sugar." Colt stood, put on his hat. Stood. "Let's go."

13

OLT

Once we rolled past the Hawk's Landing gates, I felt like I could breathe. And I wasn't the one being stalked by mentally unstable southerners. I'd been stunned when the woman had reached out and wiped the potato salad off of Lacey's hair, then prized the soiled napkin like it was the Shroud of Turin.

I needed to forget about the insanity. And if I did, then Lacey really needed to forget. She'd come to Montana to take a break and we'd give it to her. We'd make her forget everything but us.

There was one way I knew to distract her.

"Panties off, sugar."

She rode between us in my truck. While we'd taken her back to her cabin to toss a few clothes into a bag—this time for more than a quick horseback ride—she hadn't changed out of her pretty sundress.

"What?" she asked, glancing up at me. Between us, she seemed so small. So fucking perfect. I wanted her like this, riding between us down the bumpy Montana back roads the rest of our lives.

"Take them off."

"Why?"

"Because I want you spending your

time wondering when we're going to toss that pretty dress up and fuck you."

Her cheeks flushed and her eyes went soft.

"Oh."

Micah's hand found the hem and slid it up over her knee, worked it up her thigh as she lifted her hips, worked the scrap of lace down and off. I took them from her, stuck them in my shirt pocket. "Now show us that gorgeous pussy while we drive. That's it," I added when she widened her knees and had the dress bunched up around her waist. "A million times better than the view out the window."

Once we got to my property, I showed her around, the big house that was under construction. I'd walked away from the framing once I saw her for the first time. Now, seeing her here in front of the start of the house, telling her of my plans for it, I wanted to get it done as soon as possible.

"I'm building it big for a family," I told her.

Micah was quiet, watching her. Going from a wild night together to a conversation about a house I was building—for her, even when I hadn't even met her yet—to really forever was a big leap. Especially for a non-Bridgewater woman. And a woman who'd been jaded by people for years.

"Your property, it's beautiful. And you're right, it's prettier than any spot I've ever seen."

I grinned at that. I felt...full. Full of pride, full of happiness and oddly enough, full of love. This woman, shit, this woman made me feel like there was more to life than a piece of land and a dream. She was what we'd been waiting for, what had been missing. Had Fate put her in our path?

I shrugged. I didn't fucking care as long as she stayed.

"I'm living in this cabin, for now." I pointed to the smaller house set back in the woods. I'd keep it when the big house was finished, perhaps use it as a guest house. "Let me show you the inside."

She looked at me sideways. "I know what that means."

Micah stepped up to her, slid a hand up beneath the hem of her dress. "Oh?"

"It means you want to have your way with me."

"Damn straight. Are you on the Pill, sugar?" I asked.

She nodded, her eyes falling closed because Micah was touching her with his fingers. I couldn't see because her dress was tucked over his wrist, but I could imagine. I also imagined she was wet and ready for us. Again.

"Good girl. We're both clean so those condoms you packed? We won't need them. This time we'll take you bare."

"Oh god," she moaned.

"We're going to fill you up," Micah murmured. "Again and again. Mark you. You won't have any doubts who you belong to."

"And the lube?" I added. "We'll use it. And I've got a little plug to get you all ready for us."

"That's a lot of talk," she murmured, gripping Micah's forearm.

He growled, tossed her over his shoulder and carried her toward the cabin. He swatted her ass on the way. "You think we talk too much? I'll give you something to keep you quiet."

For the next twenty-four hours, she didn't say much of anything besides "More" and "Please" and "Yes!"

———

LACEY

My cell phone rang when I was on the couch with Micah. We were like two spoons in a drawer, napping. They'd kept me up all night, taking turns fucking me. Instead of using their fingers for their fun ass play, they'd pulled out a silver butt plug with a bright pink jewel on the handle. They'd played with it during the night, working it inside me, then fucking me while I wore it, but they'd pulled it out when they finally let me sleep. No, when I'd finally passed out from orgasms.

But this morning, they'd bent me over the sofa and put it in again, this time telling me to wear it for the morning.

I knew what that meant—besides walking a little awkwardly. They planned to fuck me together. At the same time. Not just sucking one of them while the other fucked me. No, I was going to be between them, one of them in my pussy, the other in my ass.

They'd said it was the ultimate claiming, that they'd do it only when I agreed I was theirs.

Until then, they didn't give me one minute when I wasn't reminded they wanted to keep me. One of them was always with me—except for a few minutes alone in the bathroom—touching me, hugging me, kissing me. Holding me like Micah was now.

It had been a full day of making out. Fooling around. Fucking.

Colt had kept his word. I had forgotten about everything but the two of them. Or what the three of us could be. I felt safe and protected. Loved, even. I liked it and wanted it to continue.

I didn't understand it, but I didn't have to. At least not right now. I'd just been myself with them and I wanted more.

Did I want forever? I had no idea, but the idea held promise.

Then my cell phone brought everything back, reminded me there was a real world and it was waiting. I went over to retrieve it from my bag.

"Lacey? Oh my god, are you okay?" Ann Marie's voice was loud through the phone.

Micah sat up and put his arm over the back of the couch as he watched me. He was shirtless since I was wearing it. I wore his shirt and nothing else—but the plug.

"Yeah, why?"

"You haven't seen the papers, have you?"

"No." All calmness washed away like

a creek in a flash flood. "Why? What are they saying?"

"Look, I called Hawk's Landing. I spoke to the owners. They know you're with your hot cowboys. One of them is coming to you."

"Jeez, Ann Marie, is Mom okay?"

"Mom's fine. It's you I'm worried about."

"I'm fine. I've been with Colt and Micah." She was quiet. "Tell me."

I heard her take a deep breath. "There are pictures. Of you."

My heart leaped into my throat. Ann Marie had been telling me the latest tabloid news for years but I'd never heard her talk like this. Usually, she was laughing. An alien baby, that kind of thing. But this time? I was scared.

Micah was eyeing me closely.

"There are pictures of you. In a lake. With a guy."

My mouth fell open, remembered the only time I'd been in a lake. Ever. And it had been with Micah. Naked. Fucking.

"That's not all," she continued. "There's another of you. Um...god, this is bad."

"What?"

"You're bent over a big boulder and a guy is behind you. You're having sex."

My fingers went numb and I felt all the blood drain from my face. Micah stood, came around the couch. I held out my hand. Stopped him.

"That was...um, yesterday. Here, at Colt's property."

"Yeah, it looks like you're enjoying yourself," she said, her voice laced with sarcasm. "The headlines are bad. 'That's Not Chris!' is one of them. Another is 'Lacey Ropes A Cowboy' and another is 'Vampire Slut'."

"Oh my god," I whisper. "How—"

"I don't know how the pictures were

taken or by whom. But Lacey, honey, you need to get out of there."

"Yeah, okay." My voice was hollow and so was my heart. I walked to the bathroom, and the last thing I saw before I shut the door was Micah's worried look.

I sat on the edge of the tub, remembering the more upbeat conversation I'd had sitting on a different tub only the day before.

"Look, Matt is coming to get you. I've arranged for a plane to bring you here."

"I'm not going to Hawaii."

"Lacey, I'm back in LA. We left early because of this. I was going to come to you, but Matt said he'd take care of you, get you home."

Home. Where the hell was home now? My house had been trashed by Chris. I rarely stayed there, and when I did, it was empty. Cold. I'd thought, maybe, I could make Bridgewater home. With Micah and Colt.

"Oh shit," I whispered.

"What?"

"The first picture, of the lake? It was up in the mountains when we were stuck from the storm. No one knew where we were going, no one but Micah and Colt."

"Are you saying one of them took the picture?"

"Colt was on the porch. Watching. He...he had a cell phone. He'd said he called the front desk to let them know where we were, that we were safe and the cabin was being used. He could have taken it."

Micah knocked on the door. "Are you okay, Lacey?"

My heart skipped a beat. "Talking to my sister!" I called back.

"I'm going to go get Colt," he replied.

I heard his heavy footsteps across the wood floor and out the front door. Colt had gone out earlier to work on the framing of the new house. The footprint for it was large, and although I'd never seen a blueprint, I knew it would be two stories with the bulk of the windows facing the mountains that were close enough to reach out and touch.

"They said they wanted forever with you," Ann Marie said.

I tried to swallow, but there was a huge clog in my throat. It hurt, ached and tears burned my eyes, then fell.

"Yeah, they did." I stood, wiped my cheeks with unsteady fingers. "Look, I have to go."

"You'll wait for Matt?"

"Of course. It's not like I can go anywhere unless I steal Colt's truck."

"Okay. Call me back. And soon. I love you, sis."

I didn't respond, only ended the call and tried to pull up the worst tabloid web site on the small screen. It was hard to see and I wiped my eyes again, and again.

There it was. On the top of the main page. It was of me and Micah in the lake. His face had been obscured with a blurring tool. My butt was blurred, too, to meet FCC guidelines, but not my face. No, that's what people wanted to see. It was salacious enough. There was no question I was naked and that we were fucking. My legs were wrapped around Micah's waist and you could see the curve of his ass.

I scrolled down. The next picture was just as Ann Marie had warned. It had been taken yesterday afternoon. After Micah had carried me into Colt's cabin and had their way with me, Colt had walked me around the construction site. When he'd finished, he'd said he couldn't wait any longer to have me again and bent me over a big rock. I'd been in Colt's shirt—they liked it when I wore them and nothing else—and my sandals and so it had been easy for him to open his pants and fuck me.

God, I'd been so naïve. So dumb to think they wanted me.

I heard a car engine, the crunch of tires. Matt. I'd never met the ranch owner, but I was glad he was here.

I stormed out of the bathroom and found my bag, pulled out a pair of jeans.

All at once I realized I had a stupid butt plug in my ass. I dashed back into the bathroom and carefully—with a whole lot of wincing—tugged it free and dropped it in the trash can. I clenched down, my body sore. Now a reminder of how stupid I'd been. How dirty I felt at the games they'd played with me. They'd said they'd claimed me. Claimed, my ass!

I had to laugh at that as I tossed on a pair of jeans. Dropping to the floor, I grabbed my sandals that had fallen beneath the side of the bed. Tugged them on. Grabbing my bag, I went outside, squinted into the bright sun.

Matt was dark like Colt, but that was where the similarities ended. He was an inch or two taller than Micah, but wide shouldered, lean hipped. He saw me before the others did, tipped his hat.

"Ma'am." He walked over to me. "I'm Matt from Hawk's Landing. I'm sorry we haven't met before now, and I'm sorry we aren't doing so under better circumstances."

"Matt told us what's going on," Colt said. My heart lurched. He was covered in sawdust, his short hair slicked with sweat. He looked completely edible, all male and gorgeous. But that didn't mean he wasn't a two-timing, conniving asshole.

I told him that. His eyes widened.

"And you," I pointed at Micah. "I believed you. Every word."

"Sugar, what are you talking about?"

"The pictures. You took them. Sold them."

Both men looked instantly stunned, then angry.

"You don't think—" Micah began, but I stopped him by stomping over, holding my phone out.

"I do think. How else would there be pictures of us? Fucking."

Out of the corner of my eye, I saw Matt stiffen, but I ignored him and the embarrassment that went along with him learning what should have been private. It didn't matter. My sex life was in full color for the entire world to see. Matt was only one person out of millions.

Micah took the phone, turned so the screen was shielded by the sun. "Fuck!" he shouted.

Colt came over, took it from him, scrolled down.

"We didn't do this," he said, his voice deadly.

"So there just happened to be photographers lurking in the trees at the cabin? How did they know there would be a storm, that we'd veer to it? That we'd even fuck?

"Sugar, we would never—"

I closed my eyes, blocked him out. I couldn't look at them anymore. The tears fell now. I wasn't very good at being angry. I was more sad, usually, and that kept me from fighting. Like now. I was done. It was just like usual.

"At least Chris—the rocker ex-fiancé —didn't take pictures. Hell, we didn't even have sex. He used me, yeah, but only for growing his fan base. I knew what I was getting into. But this? I believed your lies. All of it."

"I don't like what you're insinuating," Micah said, his voice hard.

"I'm not insinuating," I countered.

"You said forever." I choked on the word and started to cry.

"And we meant forever."

I sniffed, wiped my cheeks, settled into my actress mode. It was time to fake it. To get out of here, as far away from them as I could. I took a deep breath, even formed a smile. It almost hurt to do it, but I pasted it on. I would get a damn Emmy for this role.

"Past tense. Why did you do it? Money? The pictures got you the money you needed to finish your house, right?" I glanced from Colt to Micah. "And you? What did you need, some start-up funds?" I shrugged. "I hope you got enough. I know those tabloids drive a hard bargain. You could have just asked me for it. I have enough for whatever you want to do. You didn't even need to bare your ass to get it."

I walked toward Matt's truck. He'd thankfully remained silent through all this. He grabbed the strap of my bag from my shoulder, took it from me.

"That's it? You accuse us of selling pictures of us having sex to the tabloids and then you walk away. You don't want to find out the truth? To fight for us?" Micah asked.

I didn't turn back. "I only fight if there's something worth the battle."

"It could have been you," Colt countered. "Hiring someone to follow you, to take pictures, to end whatever fucked up relationship you had with your ex. Maybe you used us."

Those words had me turning. The sharp bite of them. Both Micah and Colt stood there, breathing hard, their faces flushed with anger.

"Just as my sister said, I needed to get laid. I'd say we're even, don't you?" I gave them one last look, then ran for Matt's truck. He was there to open the door. "Can we hurry?" I asked.

He nodded, gave the men a dark stare as he went around to the driver's side.

He didn't linger, but drove off before I could start to cry. I caught one last glimpse of Micah and Colt, the two men who'd stolen every ounce of trust I had left, but also my heart.

14

$\mathcal{M}$ICAH

After Matt drove away, Colt and I stood there, like idiots, staring at the settling dust.

"What the fuck just happened?" I asked, running my hand over the back of my neck.

I wore just my jeans as the woman of our dreams drove away, hating us.

"Someone posted pictures of us. Shit,

they're bad," Colt said. Each word he bit out as if spitting nails. "We need to go after her."

I shook my head. Every molecule in my body wanted to jump in Colt's truck and chase her, but she wasn't going to listen. Not now. We had to let her go.

"Fuck. No." I explained my reasoning and he grudgingly agreed. "We know we didn't do it, so we have to find out who did."

"Damn straight."

Colt walked toward the cabin, the cabin that still had Lacey's floral scent in the air. He grabbed his phone, settled on the couch and ran his finger over it.

"It could have been that couple from the barbecue. They were insane. They'd mentioned selling that damned napkin for a hundred dollars. Maybe they wanted more."

"Yeah, but who knew we were up at the backcountry cabin? Lacey was right.

Even we didn't know we were going there. Seriously, who could predict a fucking act of God?"

He didn't look at me as he talked, but at his cell.

"They paint her as a slut. Two men in two days. There's no question what we're doing with her."

"Do they mention us taking her together?"

He read quietly. While I wanted to sit beside him and read at the same time, the phone was too damn small.

"No. Nor our names. Only hers. We're the 'mystery cowboys' who wanted a turn at the rodeo."

"Fuck," I growled. I pinched the bridge of my nose. "You really don't think she paid paparazzi to follow her and take pictures, do you?"

He groaned. "No. She's not like that. But I was angry and I wanted her to see her accusations were ridiculous. That there were other possibilities. Instead, I made her think I was an asshole. That she'd be the petty bitch she tries so hard to avoid."

"Yeah, that kind of backfired."

"Not only do we have to find the fuckers who did this and kill them, then we'll have to make it right with Lacey."

Not a small order. I knew nothing about fame or LA or anything crazy like this shit. But Matt did. He'd been a professional baseball player. He could help. I shared my thoughts.

"Yeah, he can help. So can Lacey's sister."

"She's the one who called, who arranged for Matt to come here."

"Then she's protective. We need to get her on our side."

Colt stood, grabbed his keys. "We need to go get our girl. Make this right. Prove to her we love her. Then we'll claim her so she never forgets. If we have to get the tabloids involved—with the truth—then we'll do it."

"Abso-fucking-lutely."

———

LACEY

"You have to go back to work next week," Ann Marie said, shoving a piece of popcorn in her mouth. We were on the couch in her great room watching Sixteen Candles.

"Why can't I have a Jake Ryan?" I asked, swooning over the hero in the 80's teen flick.

"I know," Ann Marie agreed. "He's gorgeous. And the Porsche doesn't hurt him at all. You had two Jake Ryans."

She hadn't mentioned either Micah's or Colt's name since I'd been back in LA. She'd arranged for a private jet to bring me from Montana, not telling my PR firm or anyone else, not knowing who'd taken the photos. Matt from Hawk's Landing had been really nice, intentionally quiet the entire ride into Bozeman. He'd promised he would look into the breach of guest privacy and would get back to me. I hadn't heard from him yet.

I also hadn't looked at any newspapers, tabloids or even gone online. Ann Marie had gladly taken my cell and I avoided every computer in her house. She'd told me one of the papers had an article that Chris had moved on. He was old news. How he did with his band was up to him now, or whichever actress he glommed onto next.

I hadn't gone to my own place. I had no interest. After the party Chris had thrown, I had no idea the condition. Gabe had been great. He'd had a team from his company go in and pack up my personal effects; clothing and the like and bring it here. He'd then worked with a Realtor to put the house on the market.

I wasn't going back. Not just to my big, empty house across town, but to Chris. Or my job. Since we'd finished filming the end of the season, my contract was up and my agent had yet to send me papers to extend. Everyone had assumed I would return when filming began next week, me included. But my time in Montana had changed everything.

"Yeah, two Jake Ryans," I agreed. "But for only two nights. It was just a fling."

Ann Marie turned her head toward me. "You can lie to yourself all you want, but I see how you are. Those guys were more than a fling."

Gabe came into the room, holding out the house phone. "It's Matt from Hawk's Landing."

He was silent as he waited for me to

decide if I wanted to talk to him. It was my choice; they'd spent the week allowing me to decide what contact I wanted to make with the outside world.

Gabe was a few years older than me, handsome in an urban way. Dark haired, he wore a crisp business suit as he'd just gotten home from the office. I used to find him appealing, but no longer. He wasn't Colt or Micah. I didn't want the stiff corporate type. No, I wanted my cowboys.

I glanced at the phone, knew that whatever Matt was going to say wasn't bad because Gabe had screened it for me.

I took it, tucked my feet beneath me on the sofa. "Hi, Matt."

"Lacey. I assume you haven't seen the news. Or the tabloids." The last word he spit out as if it tasted bad.

"No."

He sighed through the phone. "We

discovered the identity of the person who took the photos. He was an employee, a temporary summer worker who overheard the call the men made to the registration desk letting us know you three were safe at the backcountry cabin. I guess he recognized you at check-in and decided to stalk you."

I cringed at that word. Hated it. It meant bad intentions.

"He was working the barbecue and witnessed the altercation with the enamored couple. Watched you leave with Colt and Micah. He said he followed you, took the pictures at Colt's spread."

Ann Marie was looking at me expectantly.

"They didn't do it," I said to her. Oh. My. God. They didn't do it. "I said such awful things."

"You did," Matt confirmed. "The situation was bad, Lacey. You were justified in your thoughts based on your history."

"Wait. How did the guy get to the backcountry cabin? I mean, did he take a horse? We didn't see him."

"Actually, there's an access road a few hundred yards from the cabin. It was originally made to get the building materials to the site, and it was kept not only for safety, but to maintain the cabin. A team goes up and cleans, resupplies after guests leave."

That made sense. From what Colt had said about all parts of the property cell phone accessible, this wasn't much of a surprise.

"Oh."

"As a friend—at least I'd like to think we're friends—I want to apologize for what happened. Women should be protected, not shamed or sold for salacious gain. As owner of Hawk's Landing, I would understand if you chose to sue us for the breach of privacy. I've already given our lawyer's information to Gabe."

"Oh, um. That's not necessary."

"Don't be hasty in your response. You have a right to damages as we were at fault."

"No, the guy who took the pictures was."

"You can be confident in knowing he is no longer an employee, that our lawyers have sued his ass for breach of contract, NDA and other paperwork he signed at hiring. He is also being arrested for selling inappropriate photos without consent."

"I didn't know you can do that."

"I can't say that the charges will stick, but there's nothing wrong with scaring the crap out of him in the meantime."

I had to laugh at that.

"Thank you for letting me know."

"You're welcome. If there's not anything else, I'll let you—"

A thought struck me. "You didn't fire Colt, did you? It wasn't his fault."

The words fell from my lips with a harsh breath of relief. They didn't do it. It wasn't either Colt or Micah's fault. They hadn't sold me out.

"He wasn't working at the time of your...incident, therefore has broken no employment rules. What you do in private is none of my business. As for what happened on Colt's ranch, I would assume he will be filing charges of his own for trespassing and a few other things."

"Good. Good for him."

"Take care, Lacey. If you ever wish to come to Hawk's Landing again, please contact me personally."

I offered him my thanks and hung up. There wasn't more I could say. His guest ranch had technically made a huge mistake and I paid the price. He could do nothing more than apologize and pay any money I wanted if I sued. He didn't deserve this mess any more than the rest of us.

"Well?" Ann Marie asked. While I'd been talking, she'd paused the movie and Gabe had slid in to sit beside her, pulling her into his side.

I told her about the employee, what he'd done.

"We can talk about suing Hawk's Landing another time," Gabe said. I had no doubt his firm had a whole floor of lawyers. "As for the tabloids that purchased the photos, I've gone ahead and sued them. Slander and other things. Big lawyer words I can't even remember. There will be a retraction tomorrow. While it won't take the paper versions of the stories out of circulation and people may not believe it, the photos are off the web sites."

"It won't matter," I said. "The damage is done."

"They blocked out Micah and Colt's face and kept yours. They were intentionally harming you, personally."

I shook my head. "They can write a retraction, but I don't want them writing the truth. If they do, they'll find I'm in love with two men and I won't see Colt or Micah hurt. I've done enough to them already."

"You're in love with us?"

I spun about, knocking the cordless phone to the floor. There stood Micah and Colt just inside the doorway.

They looked so good. Big and hot and perfect. Yet I could see they looked tired, weary even.

"What are you—"

They stepped into the room, blocked the big TV over the cold fireplace. "You're in love with us?" Colt asked again.

"I'm sorry," I said, my voice at first a whisper. I said it again. Louder. "I'm sorry. I'm so, so sorry."

I couldn't stop saying it because I was. The words I'd said, the accusations. I ached to go to them, but they wouldn't want me. I'd thrown them under the tabloid bus and fled.

"That's not what we want to hear, sugar."

Gabe stood, pulled Ann Marie to her feet. She looked equally parts stunned by the sight of them and equally enthralled. It was obvious she knew nothing of their presence. As for Gabe, I knew he was in on this. Matt, too. "Let's give them some space, doll." She gave me a reassuring smile before her husband tugged her out of the room.

Colt and Micah came around the huge coffee table and sat on either side of me. I felt their heat, breathed in their scent, absorbed their presence. It was like a heavy rain after a drought. I needed to be with them.

"This is insane."

Micah cracked a smile. "You've been saying this all along. Yet you say you love us."

"Right?" Colt added.

I glanced at both of them. So strong. So perfect. I nodded.

"Say it, sugar."

I cleared my throat, pushing down tears. "I love you."

They both relaxed then as if they'd been waiting for it, needing it to survive. They grinned and I couldn't help but smile, too.

Micah pulled me to him, actually tugged me onto his lap, tipped my chin up and kissed me. It was so good. Sweet and hot, my body awakened to his touch. He groaned and I whimpered.

"My turn." Colt lifted me onto his own lap, kissed me. Tongue was involved. Plenty of it. I wanted them to toss me down on this couch and have their way with me, but they had other plans. Plans that involved...talking.

"You heard Matt," Colt asked, brushing back my hair.

"That it wasn't you," I replied.

"That's right."

"I...I knew it wasn't you, yet I was so angry, so upset that the words just came out."

"We know. And I said some things that were hurtful. I didn't mean them." Colt tipped my chin up. "Will you forgive me?"

"Yes," I exclaimed, wrapping my arms around him, holding on tight.

"We came here to claim you, Lacey. You can't get rid of us that easily."

I turned my head so I could look at Micah, but Colt wouldn't let me move from the hug. "Easily? You mean a stalker and tabloid sex photos?"

"Yeah, so if we can handle something that simple, we can survive anything. As long as we're together, right?"

I laughed at his sarcasm. "Right. Your careers, your lives must be turned upside down. I mean, your parents must be hiding in embarrassment."

Micah ran a knuckle down my cheek, seemingly unfazed by the very embarrassing exposure. "We're not seventeen. We're grown men. I think all our parents know we have sex. They're just glad we're having sex with The One."

"Oh."

"Everyone in Bridgewater is waiting to meet you."

I frowned. "Me? Or Jane Goodheart?"

"You. The woman who is so important to us that we'd put it all out there on national media."

"International," I countered. "Don't forget, I'm very popular in Korea."

Micah laughed and I felt the rumble of Colt's chest.

"They want to meet you, the woman we're going to marry. The woman who stole the hearts of Colt and Micah."

"Stole your hearts?" I asked. My own was beating out of my chest.

They nodded, before kissing me again. I loved being shared by them.

"How is this going to work?" I wondered.

"You don't shoot your show all year, right?" Colt asked. He didn't give me a chance to respond. "Even though you're successful on your own with your career and we're possessive bastards, we won't stifle your dreams. But we will make you fire your PR firm. They suck. You won't be going on any international tours either. No press shit. Just do the job and come home."

"To us."

"I don't want that," I said.

Micah frowned, tensed.

"My contract is up for negotiation. I'll work it so I can live in Montana. With you. I'll come here and stay with Ann Marie for shooting, but I think the writers can work me out of the show."

"But you're Jane Goodheart and immortal now that you're a vampire. I say you kill off Kade. He's an asshole."

I stared at Colt wide eyed.

"What?" he asked. "We watched the show. All of the episodes. We love you, as Lacey and as Jane."

"You're a really good actress," Micah added. "We can role play anytime you want. I'm thinking sexy librarian."

I couldn't help but laugh. "I can do that."

"Can we get out of here now? There are too many people."

I cocked my head to the side at Colt's question. "Ann Marie and Gabe will give us privacy."

He shook his head, kissed the tip of my nose. "No, sugar. Not this house, LA. Your brother-in-law has a plane ready for us. To take you home."

"Will you come with us?" Micah asked.

I didn't have to think twice. "Yes. Take me home."

15

 OLT

I didn't give a shit about money. I had enough to purchase my land and I was patient in building my house. I had simple needs. But I could get used to the private jet. While I had no idea exactly how much money Lacey had, she was certainly a millionaire. I knew, from those damned tabloid magazines, how much she made an episode. Unless she was an idiot with her finances, she didn't need to work. It wasn't her money that funded our trip back to Montana, but Gabe. Her brother-in-law was as eager to see Lacey happy as we were.

Well, maybe not quite as much. But he was probably eager to get her out of his house. I understood his interest in getting his new wife all to himself. Once he offered his help in getting Lacey back, I looked him up online too. I'd been on technology more in the past week than I ever wanted. I was just looking forward to returning to quiet. With Lacey.

And doing it via private jet only made it all the better.

We could have inducted ourselves into the Mile High Club on the way, but I wanted no one around when we fucked her next. Not even a flight attendant. So she'd settled between us in the luxurious seats and we'd made out like teenagers.

By the time we drove back to

Bridgewater and to Micah's house in town—it was closer than my cabin—we were all beyond eager.

"I want you too much to pretend to be a librarian," she murmured as I tugged her behind me up the front steps. Micah unlocked the door and turned on the light—it was after ten and the sun had set an hour ago—and waited for us to clear the door, kick it shut and lock it.

"No pretending," I said as I stopped in front of Micah's big bed.

He closed the bedroom door, too, even went over and lowered the blinds on the windows. The idea of someone watching us have sex not once, but twice, made me want to go to the jail and beat the shit out of the guy...again. I'd punched him. Matt had let me get one good swing in before they hauled him off the ranch and to jail.

While we would never be inhibited with Lacey, neither Micah or I were exhibitionists. I didn't want anything we did seen by anyone else. I wasn't ashamed. I was protective. And after what we'd been through, very protective.

"Tonight, we want you. All of you. You said you love us. Yes?" I asked.

She nodded, but knew we wanted the words since she said, "Yes."

"Like you said, this has happened fast. Really fast," Micah said. "We have all the time in the world to get to know each other. Did you know I hate cilantro?"

Her eyes widened and her mouth fell open. "Um, no."

"One more thing you know about me then. We want to marry you, Lacey Leesworth," he told her. "Don't worry, I wasn't asking. You'll know when we ask." I saw the heated gleam, knew I couldn't wait for the right time to do so. "Tonight though, we're making you ours. Taking you together."

"Claiming you," I added. "And we'll take our time to get to know each other, outside of the bedroom too."

"Okay," she murmured. Her eyes were bright, her lips plump and red from our kisses. She'd had on a t-shirt and shorts in LA and hadn't changed. The air was cooler here and it was time to warm her up. And I didn't mean with a sweater. "But you should know, I don't like country music."

I laughed at her revelation. I hated country music, but I knew Micah had a station programmed into his truck's radio. "Fine by me," I said. "Tell me something else, sugar. Are you wet for us?"

I was done making small talk. I would tell her I didn't screw the lid back on the toothpaste another time.

Lacey's fingers went to her shorts, undid the button and slid down the zipper. After she pushed the garment off

her hips—taking her panties with it—
she raised a brow and said, "Why don't
you find out?"

Oh yeah, she was the woman for us.
There was no doubt in my mind. And
when I looked to Micah, in his either.
She was ours.

———

LACEY

I wouldn't think about Colt's words, that
they wanted to marry me. That was for
another time. I'd just gotten them back.
I'd spent a week crying, mad and sad
and everything in between. Now I
wanted to be with them, between them
again. To know that there was nothing
between us. They understood the
insanity of my job, what being with me
entailed. They knew the worst. How

much worse could it be to have sex pictures up for everyone to see? I dreaded the day I met their parents because of the scandal. Perhaps that was why they said they wanted to marry me, that I'd have a ring on my finger before we did so.

There was no pretense now. No worries. I could be myself with them. Always. They'd never known me any other way. And so I'd shucked my shorts, stripped off my panties and waited for them to pounce.

They did. It took them all of two seconds. With two big men, I wasn't sure who lifted me, who put me on the bed, who stripped off my shirt and bra with expert skill—and haste. All I knew was that between one breath and the next, I was naked, both of them were looming over me and a hand was pressed against my pussy.

"She's wet," Micah growled.

He slipped a finger inside of me and curled it as he rubbed my clit. I grabbed hold of their arms and arched my back. The touch was ruthless and precise, not a teasing touch, but one that brought me to the brink of an orgasm within a minute.

"You'll come, Lacey. We need to see it. Hear it. I need to feel you squeezing my finger. Dripping on my palm."

Micah's dirty talk was my undoing. I couldn't resist them, couldn't hold back from the pleasure he was wringing from me.

I cried out, clenched down, milking his finger, wishing it was bigger, deeper. More.

When the pleasure ebbed, he slipped from me, but I wasn't given a reprieve. "My turn," I heard Colt say just before he pushed my thighs wide and put his mouth on me.

I was so sensitive already, barely

recovered, that it didn't take much to get me to come again.

And again.

Only when I was mindless, boneless and completely at their mercy did they move me. Colt settled on the bed lying on his back and Micah positioned me over him. "Ride me, sugar," Colt growled.

I was confused. The last time I had my eyes opened, he was clothed. Now he was naked and hard, his cock curving straight up toward his belly. When he gripped the base in his fist, I watched as a drop of fluid seeped from the tip. I lowered my head to taste it, but he pushed me back up.

"Nope. Not a chance. I'll blow before I even get in your mouth. Later. I promise you can suck me off later."

I went up on my knees, hovered over him until I felt him settle at my entrance, then I lowered down. I was so wet and ready he slid in easily. I rode him with abandon, circling and shifting my hips with the pleasure, but I knew I wasn't alone in this. His hips lifted to meet me, to fill me completely. His hand gripped my hip.

I glanced over my shoulder at Micah, thinking he was missing out, but he had the lube in his hand and was dribbling it onto his fingers, coating them.

"Come here, sugar," Colt said. "Give Micah some room."

I leaned down, pressed my breasts into Colt's chest, the soft hairs there tickling my soft skin. He cupped the back of my head, kissed me. And didn't stop. Not when Micah started talking dirty, not when Micah started playing.

"You took the plug so well last week. I'm going to claim you here tonight, but I'll get you ready first." He didn't stop the litany of words. Praise, carnal suggestions, plans. Everything as he worked one finger deep into me, then another. When he scissored them open, I gasped against Colt's mouth, but he didn't stop kissing me as if he needed it to breathe.

I had no idea how much time had passed. Colt gently thrust up and into me in a rocking motion. Enough to keep us both on the edge, but not enough to push us over. When Micah finally pulled his fingers free, I heard the sound of more lube, the slick rubbing of flesh.

"My cock next," he said. "Nice and easy. Relax, breathe and we'll make you feel so good."

Colt stopped kissing me then, watched me instead. I could tell he was making sure I was okay with this, that I was enjoying it. I had no doubt they'd both stop if I needed it, but I was hoping Micah had prepared me well.

I wanted to be with them both, to be in the middle of these two amazing men.

The broad head was there, pressing. Circling. Retreating. Pressing again. Over and over with a slight bit more pressure each time until my eyes widened, my ass opened for him and he popped in.

"Oh," I gasped. Wow, it was a lot. They were big and they were both in me.

"Okay?" Colt asked, stroking over my head.

I nodded, panted. Micah shifted in slightly and I moaned.

"She's doing fine," Colt said.

"Nice and slow," Micah confirmed. "That's it. A little more, now back. Good, push back. Yes. Do you like fucking both your men?"

Now that Micah's cock was being squeezed—probably very hard—by my not-so-virgin ass hole, he started talking really dirty. Stuff I didn't even imagine before but turned me on. They began to move in opposing motions, one in, the other out as they fucked me.

Having them separated by just a thin membrane made them stroke so deep. So much. Micah's thrusts pushed me forward, rubbing my clit over Colt's lower belly.

"I'm...it's...I'm going to come."

They'd already brought me to climax twice so far, and it hadn't felt like this. I had no idea there were so many erogenous places on my body, but they'd found them all. And I was going to burst. Explode. Ignite.

Boom.

I screamed, probably making both of them deaf, but I was lost in them. Because of them.

They picked up their pace, but were still easy with it. Micah came first, muttering something about it being too good. I felt him spurt hotly into me. He remained motionless, deep inside me until he caught his breath, then slowly pulled out.

By then, I couldn't lift my head off of Colt's chest. Our bodies were slicked together with sweat and I could hear the pounding of his heart.

Once Micah moved away, Colt flipped me onto my back and took me. Slow and leisurely, but forcefully.

"Ours, sugar."

"Yes."

He stiffened above me, plunged deep. Cried out my name as he came.

I didn't come again, I couldn't. I didn't need to. I was done. So perfectly done.

"Now that's how it's supposed to be. Anything else and it's just wrong," Micah said, returning from the bathroom with a damp washcloth.

When Colt pulled out, he took the cloth and wiped gently between my thighs.

"Perfect," he murmured. "Shit, I'm hard again."

I laughed, but my eyes remained closed. "Get me a bag of frozen peas and let me take a nap. Then we can do it again."

"Are you sore, sugar?" Colt asked.

"You put a huge cock up your ass and see if you're sore," I muttered.

I felt lips brush over my jaw. Felt the smile. "Nope, just your ass. Don't worry. We'll take care of you. Every perfect part."

I felt the bed dip, Micah settling on one side of me, Colt on the other.

"You guys aren't so bad yourself. I got my two cowboys."

"Yes, ma'am," Colt drawled.

"No lasso needed," Micah added.

I couldn't help but laugh, thinking of how Colt had roped me. Yeah, he'd caught me then, but I had to think he caught me the first time I laid eyes on them. Both of them. Bridgewater-style.

WANT MORE?

Read the first chapter of Kiss Me Crazy, book 6 in the Bridgewater County Series!

KISS ME CRAZY - EXCERPT

AVERY

"This wasn't what I meant when I'd said I'd share your hotel room." My voice came out breathless and filled with laughter. It may not have been what I'd planned, but I sure as hell wasn't complaining. Canceled flights were a pain, but I'd happily spend the night in an airport hotel if this was my reward.

My head fell back as I panted for air. Jackson's lips moved to my neck, sucking and licking as he rocked his hips into me. I couldn't miss the hard length of his cock as he pinned me between his lean body and the hotel room door. My legs wrapped around his waist and one of his big hands cupped my ass. Squeezed.

God, yes.

Jackson lifted his head to grin down at me. He still had the same boyish good looks I'd crushed over in high school when he was the star of the Bridgewater High baseball team. He'd hardly noticed me back then, but now...

Well hell, now I had his full attention. So did my nipples. And my pussy.

"Are you telling me you'd rather be sleeping at the gate, waiting for a morning flight back home?" he asked, his voice a rough rumble against my neck.

I shook my head as his free hand cupped my breast through my top. My eyes fell closed and I tried to answer him as he brushed his thumb over my nipple. "Oh shit. I'm saying...um, thank god for coincidences, snow storms and overbooked hotels."

The sharp bite of Jackson's pinching fingers on my hard tip had my eyes opening, a cry escaping my lips. My panties? Totally ruined.

His answering—and very gorgeous—smile made my belly do a backflip.

Holy shit, I was making out with Jackson Wray. In a Minneapolis airport hotel room. How did this happen? Fate?

He circled his hips, rubbing his hard cock against me and I bit my lip to stifle a whimper. "Good girl."

His mouth was back on mine, his tongue delving, his short beard soft and a little ticklish. His hands moved to the hem of my thick turtleneck, found the bare skin beneath and slid up to cup my breasts. There might have been dainty mesh and lace between his calloused palms and my hard nipples, but it didn't stop my answering moan.

"Yes," I whimpered. He'd quickly find out how sensitive they were. If he kept at it, he'd get me to come. I was most of the way there and we still had our clothes on.

"I thought I was the breast man." The low voice came from behind Jackson.

I pulled back to look over his shoulder.

Dash McPherson. How had I forgotten he was there? Oh yeah, Jackson's mind-melting kisses and his fingers plucking at my nipples.

With a heated gaze and that damned dimple that appeared when he smiled at me, Dash was even better looking now than he'd been back at seventeen. Both of them were. Dash's brown hair was a touch too long, making his chiseled features slightly less intimidating, but only slightly. And that grin. Wicked and beckoning all at once. That narrowed gaze, that dark look of desire...still made my body tremble, especially since it was aimed straight at me.

Maybe Jackson could feel my reaction because his arms tightened around me and he lifted me away from the door, spinning us about and setting me down on my feet between the two of them. "I was just telling Avery what a good girl she is for letting us take care of her tonight."

Dash laughed. "As if we were going to leave you to sleep at the gate. Not only isn't it safe, but miserably uncomfortable."

I pursed my lips. "I can't even count the number of times I've had to do that. With my job, I practically live in airports."

Dash crossed his arms over his broad chest, stretching the fabric of his thermal long-sleeved shirt. Jackson's hands settled on my shoulders and he leaned in from behind me, kissed right behind my ear. I shivered and not from being cold. "And the number of times you've gone off to share a room with two men?"

I heard the hint of anger, but it wasn't directed at me. It was his possessiveness showing. I hadn't seen him in years and all of a sudden, he was all alpha male. Well, not all of a sudden. I'd heard they were both veterinarians and ran their own animal clinic in town.

They were smart *and* gorgeous. I remembered him that way when we were in high school. But they were older now. Dash took it—possessiveness—to a whole new level. And that level made my clit throb.

"You're not *just* two men," I countered. "It's been a long time, but I know you guys. We went to high school together."

Dash just continued to study me, dark brow raised.

"You're very possessive," I replied, stating the obvious.

"Baby doll, you have no idea," he countered, stepping to me and sliding my hair back from my face. It was wild and crazy and never stayed put, even in a sloppy ponytail. "Whether we do anything tonight or not, whether you let us get you naked and get you off, you're not sleeping in the damned airport. We're done here with our conference and we'll see you safely home."

While we were stuck in Minnesota for the night, we were all heading back to Bridgewater. I'd run into them at the gate, all three of us on the same flight. The cancelled flight.

I might have been born and raised in the small Montana town, but I'd left for college and rarely went back. Not with my crazy family. But my sister's wedding wasn't something I could avoid, so here I was. Almost back to Bridgewater. Not home. Dash and Jackson considered Bridgewater home, but I didn't. I didn't really have a home. I lived out of a suitcase and lately, it had been shoved underneath a narrow bed in a *casa* in Mexico. As a travel journalist, I didn't put down roots, especially in Bridgewater.

The cancelled flight was a reprieve. A delay in returning to my fighting parents and every obvious reason why I kept leaving. While it might be December and Christmas was two weeks away, my family wasn't like a Norman Rockwell painting. I knew my parents wouldn't have a tree or any kind of holiday decorations. They didn't bother. They didn't bother to get along.

"I won't spend the night at the airport. I won't turn down your hospitality. Besides, Jackson just had a hand up my shirt and I think he left a hickey on my neck. I'm not sure how that's possible wearing a turtleneck," I grumbled, tugging at the high collar. "I think the chances are pretty good you're going to get lucky."

A wild romp with two boys I'd had a crush on in high school. And by the look of them, they weren't boys any longer. No, at twenty-seven, they were *all* men. Tall, broad shouldered. Muscled. No, *chiseled.*

I wanted them, wanted to feel the weight of them pressing me into the bed, of me holding onto the headboard as they took me from behind. As they sucked my nipples. Fingered my pussy. Hell, licked it.

I wasn't a virgin and I wasn't going to pretend otherwise. I'd been with men. Men I'd met traveling for work. Men who meant nothing to me more than a quick orgasm. After watching my parents fight for my entire childhood, I had no idea what a real relationship could be like. If it was anything like theirs, I had no interest. That was why I enjoyed the physical, but that was it. No strings. No dating.

My parents' marriage was completely abnormal for Bridgewater. Almost all marriages were solid, the husbands—yes, both of them—were possessive and very protective of their wife. Affectionate. Loving. My dad was nothing like that. Hell, he'd had a whole string of mistresses and my mom ensured she wasn't lonely. Why they stayed together after almost thirty years, I had no idea, but it was like watching a car accident, stuff strewn everywhere, people hurt and no way to make it better. I was tired of being used as a tool to fuel their arguments. That was why I stayed away. I'd stopped in for a weekend last summer on my way from Alaska to the Florida Keys between assignments, but

I'd spent more time with Aunt Louise than anyone else.

And now I was going back to Bridgewater. I was dreading every minute of it, especially the seafoam green bridesmaid dress I'd wear. My mother had emailed me a picture while I was in Mexico. Perhaps this night was a reprieve, a reprieve with two gorgeous men who I hoped would be naked very soon. A night I could remember when I was laying in my childhood bed listening to my parents fight. I had no doubt Jackson and Dash would be front and center in my thoughts as I got it on with my vibrator for months—no, years—to come.

Vibrators didn't have affairs, didn't talk back. And I wasn't the one being used.

"Lucky?" Jackson asked, hands on my shoulders, nudging me closer to the bed. His thumbs pressed gently into my back. "Lucky was finding you at the gate, that we were on the same flight. That we'll spend the night with you."

"That we'll be traveling with you back to Bridgewater," Dash added. He worked off his fleece jacket. It was freezing out, well below zero and the snow was blowing thick and sideways outside the window and yet he didn't wear anything heavier.

"As for what we're going to do to you, there's no luck involved." Jackson's cocky grin returned and damn if it didn't look mighty fine with that beard of his. While his hair was brown like Dash's, it was several shades lighter. I'd felt the softness of it as he kissed me and I wondered what it would feel like...other places. Like between my thighs. Tangled in my fingers as he got me off. And I knew he'd be able to do it. Dash, too.

I'd never slept with a guy from Bridgewater, let alone two. But if I was going to, and I was...Jackson and Dash were definitely my fantasy men and I knew tonight was going to be one wild ride. We had nowhere to go until the blizzard cleared up and the ground stop was lifted. There weren't any other hotel rooms—that's why they offered to share theirs with me—even if I wanted one.

"What are you doing in Minneapolis? What brought you to my gate?" I asked, smiling. We hadn't talked much since we walked to the connecting hotel and were able to get one room.

"Vet conference," Jackson said.

"That's right," I replied, making small talk even as I fantasy-fucked them with my eyes. "You guys opened a clinic in town, right?"

I remembered hearing that from my sister. Jackie had never left Bridgewater. Hell, she'd never even left her high school job waitressing at the local BBQ joint. We had next to nothing in common these days so our conversation consisted of her filling me in on town gossip. For once, her running commentary proved useful.

Dash nodded. Neither of them touched me, but their gazes were hot and sexy as hell.

"Enough small talk," he said.

"I agree. As Jackson said, running into each other wasn't luck. A night together, stuck in a hotel room with nothing to do." I shrugged. "Why not have a little fun while we're stranded? Like I said, I've never been with two guys before but I've definitely thought about it. Show me what I've been missing?"

"You've thought about it?" Dash's lips turned up at the corners. "I think you've got it all wrong, Jackson," he said to his friend, but kept his eyes on me. "It seems little Avery here grew up to be awfully naughty."

My knees went weak at the way he'd

said the word *naughty* so Dash wrapped an arm around me, keeping me upright. Fucking hell, I did feel naughty around these two. My brain had gone to a wickedly dirty place—between them.

Dash held me snug against his hard chest and I felt Jackson move behind me so I was sandwiched between them, their rock-hard bodies trapping me and keeping me standing.

Jackson pushed my long brown curls to the side as he nuzzled my neck as best he could with my shirt on. There was that beard tingle again. "We've been wanting to do this for a long time, sweetheart. Way back in high school even when we were just horny teenagers. You've been our fantasy girl ever since then, hot for you every time we saw you when you came home, but never imagined it happening. Until now. Fuck, yes."

I whimpered. Yup, his honesty was

pretty damned hot, especially since I didn't think I was that much of a catch. But they'd wanted me for...years? Feeling their hard cocks pressing against me, I could feel their pent-up desire to get inside me.

God, yes.

Get Kiss Me Crazy now!

GET A FREE BOOK!

JOIN MY MAILING LIST TO BE THE FIRST TO KNOW OF NEW RELEASES, FREE BOOKS, SPECIAL PRICES AND OTHER AUTHOR GIVEAWAYS.

http://freeromanceread.com

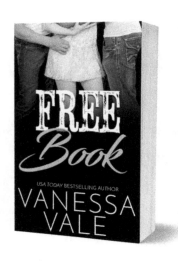

ABOUT THE AUTHOR

Vanessa Vale is the *USA Today* Bestselling author of over 50 books, sexy romance novels, including her popular Bridgewater historical romance series and hot contemporary romances featuring unapologetic bad boys who don't just fall in love, they fall hard. When she's not writing, Vanessa savors the insanity of raising two boys and figuring out how many meals she can make with a pressure cooker. While she's not as skilled at social media as her kids, she loves to interact with readers.

BookBub

Instagram

www.vanessavaleauthor.com

ALSO BY VANESSA VALE

Grade-A Beefcakes

Sir Loin Of Beef

T-Bone

Tri-Tip

Porterhouse

Skirt Steak

Small Town Romance

Montana Fire

Montana Ice

Montana Heat

Montana Wild

Montana Mine

Steele Ranch

Spurred

Wrangled

Tangled

Hitched

Lassoed

Bridgewater County Series

Ride Me Dirty

Claim Me Hard

Take Me Fast

Hold Me Close

Make Me Yours

Kiss Me Crazy

Mail Order Bride of Slate Springs Series

A Wanton Woman

A Wild Woman

A Wicked Woman

Bridgewater Ménage Series

Their Runaway Bride

Their Kidnapped Bride

Their Wayward Bride

Their Captivated Bride

Their Treasured Bride

Their Christmas Bride

Their Reluctant Bride

Their Stolen Bride

Their Brazen Bride

Their Bridgewater Brides- Books 1-3
Boxed Set

Outlaw Brides Series

Flirting With The Law

MMA Fighter Romance Series

Fight For Her

Wildflower Bride Series

Rose

Hyacinth

Dahlia

Daisy

Lily

Montana Men Series

The Lawman

The Cowboy

The Outlaw

Standalone Reads

Twice As Delicious

Western Widows

Sweet Justice

Mine To Take

Relentless

Sleepless Night

Man Candy - A Coloring Book

CPSIA information can be obtained
at www.ICGtesting.com
Printed in the USA
BVHW041636070421
604344BV00013B/1769